BOOKS BY *Robert Nathan*

NOVELS	*So Love Returns* (1958) *The Rancho of the Little Loves* (1956) *Sir Henry* (1955) *The Train in the Meadow* (1953) *The Innocent Eve* (1951) *The Married Look* (1950) *The River Journey* (1949) *Long after Summer* (1948) *Mr. Whittle and the Morning Star* (1947) *But Gently Day* (1943) *The Sea-Gull Cry* (1942) *They Went On Together* (1941) *Tapiola's Brave Regiment* (1941) *Portrait of Jennie* (1940) *Winter in April* (1938) *Journey of Tapiola* (1938) *The Enchanted Voyage* (1936) *Road of Ages* (1935) *One More Spring* (1933) *Jonah* (1925)
AN OMNIBUS	*The Barly Fields* (1938)—containing *The Fiddler in Barly. The Woodcutter's House. The Bishop's Wife. The Orchid. There Is Another Heaven.*
POEMS	*The Green Leaf* (1950) *The Darkening Meadows* (1945) *Morning in Iowa* (1944) *Dunkirk* (1941) *A Winter Tide* (1940) *Selected Poems* (1935)
THEATER	*Jezebel's Husband & The Sleeping Beauty* (1953)
NON-FICTION	*Journal for Josephine* (1943)

These are BORZOI BOOKS, *published by* ALFRED A. KNOPF

SO LOVE RETURNS

SO LOVE RETURNS

BY

ROBERT NATHAN

NEW YORK
Alfred · A · Knopf
1958

L. C. Catalog card number: 58–9673

THIS IS A BORZOI BOOK,
PUBLISHED BY ALFRED A. KNOPF, INC.

 Manufactured in the United States of America. Published simultaneously in Canada by McClelland & Stewart Ltd.

Published September 22, 1958
First and second printings before publication
Third printing, September 1958
Fourth printing, November 1958

The epigraph from THE MEADOW SONNETS *is reprinted from* THE GREEN LEAF: THE COLLECTED POEMS OF ROBERT NATHAN, *published by Alfred A. Knopf, Inc., copyright 1941, 1950 by Robert Nathan.*

To my sister, Marian Sandor,
and her husband, Paul.

Now blue October, smoky in the sun,
Must end the long, sweet summer of the heart.
The last brief visit of the birds is done;
They sing the autumn songs before they part.
Listen, how lovely—there's the thrush we heard
When June was small with roses, and the bending
Blossom of branches covered nest and bird,
Singing the summer in, summer unending.
Give me your hand once more before the night;
See how the meadows darken with the frost,
How fades the green that was the summer's light.
Beauty is only altered, never lost,
And love, before the cold November rain,
Will make its summer in the heart again.

From the Meadow Sonnets.

SO LOVE RETURNS

CHAPTER 1

THE house stood on a shelf above the sea; the empty moorlands, the desert-colored, California hills, already brown in July, rose up behind it toward the sky that was clear and pale like a mountain sky and blue as a cornflower. It was bare, gaunt country, beyond Trancas, with a few dusty eucalyptus trees here and there in the canyons. The fogs would come in until noon, and the sea would rise and fall in slow, oily motion in the kelp, and then the sun would come out and the water and the air would shine with light.

Trina, my wife, was dead. The first grief, the breathless grief you can't live with, was over, and I was settling down to work again. Our two children played on the beach below the house, they built sand-castles and gave shrill cries like sea-gulls when the waves ran up the sand at them. They seemed to have accepted the summer as they found it, without their mother; otherwise it was like other summers, except that they were older.

Trisha was not quite five when her mother died, and Chris was going on four. We had always been a warm family, close-knit and happy, and poor, the way most writers' families are. We had our own way of doing things, and after Trina died we went on doing things that way. Trisha had a little desk in my study, next to my own, and she kept her paper dolls there and worked at her cut-outs while I wrote. It wouldn't have been good for most writers, but it was good for me; I liked to have Trisha sitting there next to me, her dreamy little face bent over her work, her little blunt scissors in her hand.

Chris was different. He liked to play in the bare, sandy yard behind the house, where there were lizards to look at and treasures to find in the ground, stones, and sometimes a shell or an old bottle cap.

Lunch was a peanut-butter sandwich and a glass of milk, which Trisha got from the ice box. I cooked the dinner, and we all washed the dishes. The children said their prayers before the fireplace, and put themselves to bed; and I read to them.

I made a living, such as it was, out of children's books. I could write two or three a year, and twice I had written a novel of my own. As long as I could keep writing, we got along; but sometimes I lay awake at night, thinking of what would happen if I couldn't write. In the morning I'd be hopeful again; perhaps a book of mine would get a book-club or a prize. Nothing like that had ever come my way, but it might. Every writer has thoughts like that, all the time.

We didn't have any money laid aside, and it was understood that when one of us wanted anything out of the ordinary he had to wait until the next check came in. That's how Trisha got her paper dolls, and how Chris got his first pair of long pants. He was almost four at the time, and when he got them they were too big, and kept falling off. He cried, as he sometimes did, in a quiet, desperate sort of way; he sat in the big rocking chair, shaking his head from side to side, with the tears running down his face, and holding his pants up to keep them from falling down.

Trina was still alive then; she fixed him up with suspenders made of red flannel and string. After a while he grew into the pants, and didn't need the suspenders any more.

Now I was sitting looking out at the fog and the gray sea, and thinking about the book I was writing, and wishing I could get on with it. It was about a witch . . . a sea-witch, who lived in a cavern underneath the ocean. The trouble was, I'd made her a wicked witch, which disturbed Trisha who wanted her to be beautiful and good. I told her I only knew wicked witches, I didn't know any good ones. But the truth was, I didn't know any witches at all, and didn't believe in them, and Trisha did.

"They dance on the sand," she said, "when nobody is looking. You can see the little holes they make with their wands. And they make little feet marks, like a bird.

"They dance the minuet."

And putting down her scissors, she slid off her chair, and did a few awkward hops around the room. "Like that," she said. "That's a minuet."

"I see," I said. "Well, thank you very much."

And I turned back to my typing. At least I knew, now, that witches danced a minuet.

She climbed up onto her chair and gave her dolls a stern look. "All right," she said; "no talking or anything. My father is working.

"Everybody be quiet."

A writer finds a style, and he stays in it to the end. He may envy other writers their styles which allow them to do the bold things and see the strange places, but if his style is to stay at home, there's no use thinking about it. Perhaps Chris would grow up to try the slopes of Everest or fish the blue Caribbean, but Trisha's world and mine was a small beach and an empty sea, paper dolls, and a sea-witch who danced on the sand and left footprints like a sandpiper.

I missed having someone to confide in; not so much to help me with my problems, as to share the small pleasures and daily observations. Grief—or even trouble—is an alone sort of thing, you can't share it with anyone. But joy takes sharing, and so does love.

We had a few friends; sometimes on hot days other families came down to picnic on the beach, and other children with names I never knew played on the sand with mine. And sometimes Dick Basset dropped in of an evening. He had been a motion picture writer in the days when motion pictures were a big industry, and now he wrote for television. "The old days are over," he liked to say, "the glory has departed. Stick to your children's stories, Lenny; this is no time for writers."

He still made twenty thousand dollars a year, but he said it was hard work, and I guess he was right. I wouldn't have known how to go about it, myself.

"A writer has only one thing to sell," he used to say: "words. Words, and his own dreams. Me, I use my own words to sell other people's dreams . . . deodorants, and floor polish."

I had another friend, too, and that was Harry

Cole, or Old Uncle Harry Cole, as he liked to be called. He used to come down to the beach to fish, from his house in Nichols Canyon. He'd thread the tiny, squirming sandcrabs on to his hook, and spin his line out into the surf a good two hundred feet, beyond the breakers. Then he'd bring it back in again. Sometimes there'd be a fish on it, a perch or a small bass; more often the crab was gone or only the limp small empty shell was left. The perch were too mealy to eat, and the bass were infrequent, but Uncle Harry didn't seem to mind. "It's the casting," he explained; "watching the line go out like an arrow, into that secret water. And then waiting to find out what's there."

"It's usually a six inch perch," I told him, "and you have to get the hook out." "Well, yes," said Uncle Harry, "but it might be something else." "A six foot octopus," I said, "or a manatee."

"Hell," said Uncle Harry, "why not? You got the word, Lenny?"

I thought I knew the answer to that: I thought I had the word. "No one ever got a manatee on this beach," I said; "not yet, anyway." "You're right," said Uncle Harry. "And nobody ever went up Everest either, before last year."

So it was Uncle Harry who had the word, after all. Because I too went on casting my dreams out into that secret water. Tomorrow something would come . . . there'd be a letter from my publisher, there'd be a prize, a book-club, a bottle top . . . a six foot octopus. . . .

Chris had a little fishing rod, too, but he only caught seaweed. He soon grew tired of it. Once he caught a sea-anemone, and couldn't get the hook out. He left the whole outfit on the beach, and climbed back to the house to complain about it.

"It had things that waved," he said. "I didn't like it." I told him to put it into a pail of sea-water, and maybe it would let go of the hook itself. But it was Trisha who got the pail and filled it with water. It was always Trisha who did sensible things like that.

I think that was the way her mother had wanted it; she wanted our children to take care of themselves and of each other. I often thought that they had learned their lessons better than I had; it was hard sometimes to realize that Trina wasn't watching over me any more, and telling me what to do. She had never been possessive, only watchful. I suppose that's about as much comfort as a man can have.

She taught the children not to be afraid of anything—not to be afraid of people, or the sea, or strange dogs, or thunderstorms. She wanted them to be at home in the world, and so they were; more so than I was.

Trisha had something on her mind; like the sea-anemone, she couldn't let go of it. She sat there beside me, her blue eyes staring off into space. "I don't think you should make the sea-witch a bad person," she said at last, "just because she lives in the sea."

"Well," I said doubtfully, "she does have odd friends. Lobsters and crawly crabs. And sharks and barracudas. And a blowfish," I added, to settle the matter.

She wanted to know what a blowfish was. "It's a little fish," I said, "and it blows itself up to make itself look big."

"What does it do that for?" she asked.

I explained that it kept the bigger fish from eating it. "You mean," she said, "it's like when Chris is making himself big by yelling and stuff."

She gave me a small-girl-look. "I thought maybe it was a spidery horror," she said.

"Anyway," she said presently, "the sea-witch will fix it. She'll make the blowfish unblow itself."

Trisha's belief in the sea-witch far exceeded my own. To her, anything in a book was real, and most of all if I had written it. The result was, I spent a lot of time at the library looking up facts.

She had her favorites among the characters. There was the pirate whom I had hanged on a yard-arm somewhere off Trinidad, and good riddance, I thought, to bad rubbish. But Trisha was quite sad about it for a while. "He was bad," she admitted, "but he could have come-ye-and-repented."

I think she fancied herself in the role of the good woman. But she was too honest to be taken in very long by her own goodness. "Chris is bad sometimes, too," she said, "and I feel like I could smack him." "He isn't bad," I said, "he's naughty."

I tried to explain the difference between bad and naughty. "When Chris is naughty," I said, "he's mad because he's smaller than you. But he loves you, and if he made you cry, he'd be sorry afterwards." "No he wouldn't," said Trisha.

She thought it over for a moment, her young eyes wary and doubtful. "He only loves lizards and things," she said at last.

"He's your brother," I said. "Don't you love him?" "Yes," she said; "but he's only little. When his pants fell down, he cried."

I could see she was headed for that part of herself where a little girl keeps her virtues, to take them out and gloat over; and like the blowfish, she was ready to make herself look bigger than she was. I thought I'd change the subject. "It's better if people are bad in books," I said, "rather than at home."

Trisha was like any other woman; she detested moral lessons. "Oh pooh," she said.

"Anyways, the sea-witch isn't bad. She's just lonesome, with nothing but crabs."

I wonder if you are lonesome too, my daughter, I thought, but not out loud, because I was hoping she wasn't. After all, she had her paper dolls, and Chris, and other children sometimes, and the wide, wet sands with their tangled kelp and an occasional piece of wood or a colored stone. It was a lovely world to a child . . . or so I wanted to believe.

And of course she had her own private world,

in which the pirate, having escaped hanging, might still come-ye-and-repent; and where the sea-witch was beginning to assume a face and a body.

She saw her clearly. She was all ready to love her.

CHAPTER 2

AFTER the usual lunch of peanut-butter sandwiches, milk, and an apple, the children went down to the beach to play, and I settled back at my desk for a quiet afternoon's work. I had some letters to attend to, and a chapter of my book to finish; and I wanted time to think. Not about anything in particular; a writer's mind is a meadow in the sun, and thoughts cross it like a shadow of a cloud, or a sway of leaves.

And so I thought about my book, and about the children down there below me playing on the sand, I thought of how the hills rose up behind me, I thought of the state of the world, I thought of Trina . . . I tried to remember how we'd met, at some party, but I couldn't remember. There had been so many parties, in those days. I couldn't believe I'd never see her again. She always said I'd write a great book some day, and I always said that if I did, it would be because of her. But Trina didn't think so. She believed that every writer had a daemon who guided him through worlds of beauty and wonder he had never seen, and took him off into flights of wisdom he didn't know were there. All that was over now; if I had ever had a daemon, he left me when Trina did. I was just as sure that whatever I had done that was good or worth doing had been done because of her.

She had a way of saying How pitiful, when anyone disagreed with her. I could hear her saying it now, looking at me with wide eyes, and laughing a little, and laying her hand against my cheek, the way she always did, palm up as though to catch a few drops of mercy in it. It seemed so natural that she should be in some shadowy corner of the house, busy with household things . . . I held my breath a moment, listening. But there was nothing, only the sound of the sea outside, and in the house the sound of silence.

It is wrong to say that time passes, because it is all around us, like the sky; and we move on it like a blown leaf on a still lake, now fast, now slow. Last night is as far away as Troy, or just as near.

Troy was old before the Argive ships beached themselves on her shore; and before that, still older and greater cities had turned to dust and been forgotten. Even their names were forgotten.

Avaris, Sodom, Ur, Tarshish, Ophir, Yumne—we scarcely know where they stood. And where is Ys? At the bottom of the sea. I thought of the traitorous princess with her golden key, who had opened the gates to her lover, and let the ocean in. Trina, too, was far away. There is no distance on this earth as far away as yesterday.

Dick Basset loved Trina, just as everyone did who knew her. But he had no use for her daemon; he used to say that his own daemon only got him into trouble. "There I am," he said, "in a story-conference with my producer, and already I'm way out beyond my depth. I'm alone—I'm drowning—and where's my daemon? In the commissary, lunching with a friend." "How pitiful," said Trina. And she added, laughing, but half serious, too: "People shouldn't go too far out." "Your wife is a wise woman," Dick said to me, teasing her.

He missed her, too. As for the children, I didn't know. They rarely spoke of her, or when they did it was simply, the way they might have spoken about an absent friend. Children don't think very much about death, they accept it as something that happens; what troubles them is to lose someone's love. They never felt they had lost Trina's love.

No; death has a hard time frightening children, there is too much life in them and around them. But children miss the living presence of love in a house: a love that falls like a dew from above and which they can soak up like hungry grass. The children of a man alone can never feel, falling upon them like a balm, the tenderness of a man and a woman in love.

A man alone can't teach his son to believe in angels, or his daughter to cook. And that summer Trisha wanted to learn to cook, among other things. I bought her a little cookbook, and she learned to make Indian pudding and to heat oatmeal in a double boiler, but when it came to noodles, she almost gave up.

I found her one day, disconsolate beside the stove on which a pot full of some glutinous material was slowly bubbling. She turned her harassed, puckered little face up to me, the face of a child who feels that the grown-up world has betrayed her. "It says on the box," she declared, " 'cook until tender.' But who knows when tender is?"

Who indeed? What father can tell a little girl

when tender is? Tender is when a heart replies to the cry of another, when a mother comforts her child, when a woman turns at midnight to her lover. "I wish I knew how to tell you," I said, "when tender is."

And Chris, playing in the yard, chasing a little lizard from stone to stone, was by himself, as all children are, even in the middle of a parade or at the circus or in a game of blindman's buff. Children are used to alone-ness, it doesn't frighten them any more than death does.

Not that children can't be frightened, for the world around them is full of mystery, and out of that mystery come things that go bump in the dark. Some children frighten easily: a wave or a wasp can do it. Others are tougher, as mine were.

But it had its contrary side: a brave child is usually in trouble. Chris in particular had a way of falling out of trees and off ladders, of skinning his elbows and scraping his knees, and being stung by hornets. It never made him truly sorrowful; he might yell a little, but as long as his honor was safe, there was no real harm done. When his pants fell down, that was entirely different.

Trisha was the more solid of the two. When Trina died, she stepped, as far as she was able, into her mother's shoes, and soothed the skinned elbow and bandaged the scraped knee. It all seemed perfectly natural to Chris, who came to Trisha to have his buttons sewed on and his ears washed. I tried for a while to take over the buttons myself, but after Trisha saw how I handled a needle and thread she took the sewing out of my hands. She was six then, and handy.

I had my windows open, looking out at the sea, and I could hear the children playing on the sand below. I wished their mother could have heard them, too, wherever she was.

There was nothing to worry me about the day; the weather was mild, the air warm, the sun hot on the sand. There were not many people on the beach. There was a little breeze, but not much, and the waves were small and broke close in, which would keep Chris in water not much higher than his knees. That is, if he had any sense. In any case, Trisha was there to watch him.

I turned back to my writing. Little by little the children's voices faded away in my mind, and that sense of timelessness set in in which all horizons are lost; the writer sits in the center of the universe and nothing moves. The hours stand still; and birds and waves and children's voices, wind, leaves, and dust, crickets and distant sounds mingle and fade in a single silence.

I don't know how long it was before I heard the screams. I thought I heard Trisha's voice, and I got up fast, and my chair fell over on the floor.

I don't think I breathed as I went down the hill; I scarcely touched the ground at all. I hit the bottom in a shower of sand.

Trisha was huddled over something, and somebody was standing behind her—who or what I didn't notice. When I got closer, I saw that Trisha was huddled over Chris; he was lying with his face in the sand, and not moving. I knelt down very slowly beside her, and she looked up at me in a frightened way. "I told him not to," she said, "but he did, anyway."

I put both arms around her, and we stared down at Chris together. I had a desperate feeling that there was something I ought to do, but I didn't know what. Some life-saving trick, I thought; artificial respiration; or was it too late? I knew I had to try. I leaned over Chris's little squab-like body, and put my hands on his back; his skin was cold, and I could feel his ribs.

I could have sworn it was my dead wife's voice I heard, low and husky and sweet. "Don't be afraid," it said. "He'll be all right."

And at that moment, Chris stirred under my hands, and turned his face to look at me. "Hey," he said, "you're squashing me."

Relief made me weak, and I sat down suddenly in the sand. "Don't you ever do that again!" I exclaimed. And in a fine rage, I added:

"Getting yourself drowned!"

Trisha leaned over to me and patted my hand. "He isn't drowned," she said. "He only thought he was."

And pointing behind her, she added:

"The lady saved him. She plucked him from a watery grave."

I looked up then, but I was looking into the sun, and I couldn't see very well. I put my hand up against the light; and for one breathless moment I thought it was Trina.

It wasn't Trina. The girl was tall and slender, like Trina, but she had long hair the color of sea-drift; her eyes were gray, I thought, or perhaps green. Her hair hung down almost to her waist, and it was wet as seaweed. "Your little boy's all right," she said. "He'll be running around again tomorrow."

Now that I'd seen her, she didn't sound so much like Trina either. "Thank you," I said. It was a weak thing to say, the way I felt, but I tried to say it with all my heart. "It was nothing," she said. "He was never in danger, really."

She smiled and made a little shy gesture with her hand as though to say good-bye, and turned and walked away down the beach. I picked Chris up in my arms and we went up the hill to the house, and Trisha came along behind us.

"I saw him in the water," she said, "and I told him he'd better come in, and then a big wave came and I didn't see him any more. And then the lady came right up out of the sea, and she was holding Chris, and his eyes were closed and I thought he was drowned." "I wasn't drowned," said Chris. "I was plucked from a watery grave."

It was a line from a book I had been reading to them. "She had a kind of spear," said Trisha, "and fins on her feet." "She must have been skin-diving," I said. "She had seaweed in her hair," said Trisha, "like flowers." "That was kelp," I said. "She must have been in the kelp."

I put Chris to bed between two blankets, and gave him some hot cocoa to drink. After a while his teeth stopped chattering, and I could see there was nothing wrong with him, and he fell asleep smiling secretly to himself.

But I was still shaky, and I didn't feel like working any more. I sat at my desk and looked down at the sea, and I thought that I hadn't seen any fins or a spear in the girl's hand. She must have dropped them at the water's edge. Except that when she left, she didn't turn toward the water, but walked away, down the beach. . . .

I couldn't ask Trisha about it, because she was asleep, too. Anyway, it didn't seem very important; she had probably imagined the whole thing—the spear and the fins and the flower-like seaweed in the girl's hair. She had certainly saved Chris's life. I'd have to find out who she was, and thank her.

The sea stretched away below me, blue and shining near the shore, darkening toward the horizon. It looked cold and deep, and full of secrets; and for the first time I felt a little afraid of it.

CHAPTER 3

THAT feeling didn't last very long, and it wasn't meant to. You couldn't be afraid of the sea, standing on the beach in the bright summer weather, watching Old Uncle Harry Cole whip his line out above the breakers. The air had that fresh salt taste of ocean, and the iodine smell of kelp, and the hot smell of sand; and the little wind came cold off the water all the way from China.

I went more often to the beach those days, looking for the girl with the long, sea-drift hair and the green eyes. I wanted to thank her for what she'd done, but I couldn't find her anywhere. No one knew her, or even remembered having seen her, but she stayed in my mind. I kept thinking of her face as it looked framed against the light, and her long, wet hair, and her voice that had sounded —for a moment—so much like Trina's.

I asked Uncle Harry if he knew who she was, but he shook his head. "No sir," he said; "if there'd been somebody like that around, I'd have remarked her." I said I thought she might have been skin-diving, and had come in when she heard Trisha scream. "Now what would a skin-diver want around here?" he asked, "where there's nothing but perch?"

As the days went by, I found myself more than

ever determined to find her. I even went so far as to take my car and drive along the shore road, looking down at the houses, as though they could tell me something about her. But they were just the usual beach houses, small and blank, and they told me nothing. I didn't see her anywhere.

I dreamed of Trina a few times. I was curiously restless, pacing my room with empty thoughts, while Trisha watched me with concern across her table. She could see that I wasn't getting on with my writing, and it worried her. "When are we going to get the next check?" she asked. She had her heart set on a doll's house complete with cut-out furniture in the Victorian style.

As I looked at her in her wrinkled overalls, I realized that she and Chris were growing up. The overalls were too tight for her, and her little denim dress from last year no longer covered her knees. I ought to buy her some proper clothes, I thought: a little girl's dress, a party frock . . . the kind of things her mother would have bought. And Chris, too, needed shoes and a pair of trousers. They were growing so fast that summer.

Trisha made me tea for lunch, and brought me a peanut-butter sandwich; she wanted to know if she could do anything for me. "You're probably tired," she said, "from thinking so hard."

It made me feel guilty, because I wasn't thinking about my book at all. I couldn't write. I went for a long walk on the beach by myself, rounding each sandy point in a kind of breathless rush, and then feeling disappointed and foolish when there was nobody there.

Two days later Trisha came up from the beach with the news I'd been waiting for. "The lady," she said; "the one who saved Chris from being drowned? Well, I saw her." She made the announcement at dinner, with her mouth full of spinach. "I was standing with my feet in the water," she said, "and she looked out of a wave at me."

There was no sense of wonder in the remark; apparently to Trisha it seemed perfectly natural that a girl with long hair and sea-green eyes should look out of a wave at her. "What were you doing?" I asked, "and what did you do?" "She was doing wee-wee," said Chris. "I was not," said Trisha. "Anyway, I just waved at her."

I tried to keep back the eagerness I felt. "Did you notice where she went?" I asked. "Did she come out onto the beach, or anything?" "She went back into the sea," said Trisha.

It was disappointing, but at the same time I felt suddenly light-hearted, as though I'd lost a weight of worry. The girl hadn't simply disappeared, then—she was somewhere around, she had come out of the sea, and gone into it again, and she couldn't live far away.

I knew something else, too; I knew that whatever it was that had drawn me to search for her, drew her back to us as well; I believed I'd find her one day, and that I wouldn't be a stranger to her when I did.

And in the evening, when the children were in bed, having said their prayers, Trisha with her favorite doll on the pillow beside her, and Chris with the shell of a small crab, dried out and empty and broiled pink by the sun, I thought about this girl from the sea, about whom I knew nothing but to whom I already felt drawn in a way I couldn't explain.

There are so many mysteries in the world, from

the stars in their multitudes to the way of spiders. And the way a poet spins beauty and wisdom out of himself, that Trina called his daemon; and the hearts of children, who believe everything, and accept everything, from a lizard on a leaf to a woman in the sea.

When I told Uncle Harry Cole that Trisha had seen the woman in a wave, he expressed no surprise. "I've seen many sights along this beach," he said, "including a dead whale. When she comes in from swimming in the sea, I'll be glad to meet her." "So will I," I said.

Once, long afterwards, I told her that Uncle Harry had classed her with a dead whale, and I thought she would laugh, but she didn't. "I, too, will die in the sea some day," she said soberly, "just as others will die in the air and in the earth. It's nothing to laugh about." I remember that I didn't pay much attention to it at the time.

A few days after my talk with Uncle Harry Cole I took the children on a picnic to a rocky point a half mile or so from our cove, where people sometimes fished for bass when the tide was in. It was low tide, and no one was there. I carried a little stove made out of a tin can with holes punched in it, and Trisha carried the basket of food, while Chris was given a bottle of milk and a pail to put cold sea-water in.

The children were in high spirits; the thought of cooking their supper out-of-doors over a fire delighted them, though the fire was only in a tin can because the hills were dry and open fires were not allowed.

It was full summer, and the air was still warm in the afternoon. The children ran squealing into the surf, and jumped up and down in the foam, and I stayed on the beach and got the stove going. The sun sank slowly down the west and glinted and danced on the water; at our backs the hills rose up clear and bright against the sky's deep blue as night crept up behind them. Far out across the water the sea shone like gold.

The children came up from swimming, with wet, stringy hair and chattering teeth, and I dried them off, and they got into their clothes, and hung happily over the fire on which the frankfurters were cooking and giving off a good smell. We ate our supper in the last low golden light of late afternoon, and after that we sat around the stove and looked up at the sky and out at the sea, and the children asked me to read them a story. "I have no book," I said.

"Well, tell us, then," said Trisha. "Tell us about the sea-witch some more." "I want to hear about the pirate," said Chris.

"He told us about that twice already," said

Trisha. But that didn't make any difference to Chris. "I like it," he said. "Where he gets hanged and everything." "Well, I don't," said Trisha; "it's just boy stuff.

"Tell us about the sea-witch. Tell us about that part where she comes up out of the sea like a fog, all gray and everything, and old Triton blows his wreathed horn." "Well," I said, "she came up onto the beach, all gray and dripping, and she walked along the sand, looking for the children." "That's the part that always scares me," said Trisha happily.

"She had her friend the black whale with her," I said, "and the children knew she was there because of the footprints." "She didn't have footprints," said Trisha. "She left marks like a bird; remember?

"Tell us some more about her."

"The children were hiding," I said, "in a cave in the rock, and they held their breaths in terror." "She only wanted to play with them," said Trisha. "You told us that was only it." "Well, yes," I admitted, "but that was before. This time she wanted to take them down with her to her cave at the bottom of the sea."

I tried to make it sound as doomed and drowned as possible. Trisha wriggled herself closer to me, and held her breath. "Then what?" she said.

But Chris was getting tired, and nobody was getting killed. "Aren't there going to be any pirates at all?" he asked, and lay back and closed his eyes.

After I'd returned the sea-witch to the sea where she belonged, I covered the children with a blanket, and went for a walk along the beach. It was the time of day when I liked best to be alone;

evening was coming on, twilight was around me, and the sky in the west was a pale, clear green, like water under ice. The evening star hung there by itself, alone in the heavens. The hills were dark now, and everything was quiet. At such a time a man's thoughts about his life and his work are apt to be gentle and peaceful. The sea was dark, too, and my thoughts were peaceful and without bitterness.

After a while I found myself walking through an area of white mist; a small sea fog must have rolled in without my noticing it. It was strange, because the evening was clear, and there wasn't any other sign of fog along the coast. I hesitated a moment, wondering if I ought to go back, but at that moment the mist seemed to lift a little, and a sandpiper went by, skittering along the water's edge. I took a few steps forward and came around a pile of weedy rocks, and the girl was standing there waiting for me.

I didn't say anything, and neither did she. In the dusk her face was indistinct; she looked shadowy but at the same time familiar. We stood there staring at each other, and after a while I said:

"I wanted to thank you for what you did for us." She didn't answer, and I thought she hadn't heard me. "I'm very grateful," I said. "I tried to find you."

It seemed to reach her, in some far-off place. "I know," she said. Her voice was the way I had remembered it, low and sweet, like Trina's. "You don't have to thank me," she said, gently.

I didn't know what to say next. "Do you come often to the beach?" I asked. It sounded stiff and stupid, and she shook her head in what might have been a yes or a no. I thought she smiled, but it might have been only a shadow on her face. "Do you live here?" I asked.

She didn't answer. She made the same little gesture, half shy, half friendly, that she had used before when she left me kneeling on the sand with Chris. "It's getting late," she said. "It's time the children were in bed."

A gull swept in suddenly from the sea, with such a loud cry, and so close to my head that I ducked out of the way. When I turned around again, she was gone.

I looked in the sand for her footprints, thinking they'd tell me in which direction she'd gone. But there weren't any; all I could see were the marks of sandpipers. It was dark by then, and I could have missed them. I gave up after a while, and went back to the children. Chris was asleep, but Trisha was singing to herself.

CHAPTER 4

THERE were some days of fog after that, and we stayed close to the house. It was cold, and we had a fire going most of the time, and the eucalyptus logs made a sweet, smoky smell in the air. There was a steady drip from the roof, and the sound of the sea below us was muffled and heavy. The days were long, the hours went slowly. I finished a chapter of the book; Trisha cut out a new wardrobe for her dolls, and Chris caught a spider and put it in an empty glass where it stayed for a while and climbed out during the night.

On the third day the phone rang, and it was the girl.

I knew her voice right away; I could feel myself brighten up like a sparrow in the sun. All the coldness and the dampness went out of the world, and the house was suddenly snug and warm and smelled of wood smoke and paper dolls and paste. I must have sounded the way I felt, because I thought she pulled back a little, and there was a pause before she asked how the children were. I told her they were fine. She sounded shy, and I could tell that she was embarrassed. "I wish I knew your name," I said. "Who are you?"

She seemed to hesitate a moment, as if she were

making up her mind, and then she said, "I'm Kathleen."

"Is that your name?" I asked; "Kathleen?" "Yes," she said. "Is that all?" I asked, and she said "Yes." "It's an Irish name," I said. "Are you Irish?" "No," she said.

I told her that I had kept the children at home because I was afraid they might get chilled on the beach. "I know," she said; "I looked for you." The way she said it was grave, but a little breathless, like a young girl, and I put a lot of warmth into my voice when I answered her. "We'll be there to-morrow," I said, "come rain or shine." "There'll be no fog tomorrow," she said. "The weather will be fine."

It never occurred to me to wonder how she knew. "Will you be there?" I asked, and she said Yes, she thought so.

The next morning the sun came out bright and hot as she had said it would. She was waiting in the cove when we got there, a young, slender figure just as I had remembered her; she wore a bathing suit of some green material that looked like fish scales, and her hair was piled up on her head and caught in a loop of kelp. She was prettier than I had remembered, though perhaps pretty isn't the right word for it; there was a delicate beauty about her face that made me think of a shell long polished by the sea. Her eyes, when she looked out over the water, were green, but it might have been the reflection of the waves for when she turned to smile at the children or at me they were gray. Her arms and legs were the color of ivory; there was no tan, no mark of the sun on her. I remember thinking it strange at the time.

The children went to her at once, as though

she were an old friend. Chris had to tell her about his spider which, to listen to him, must have been at least six inches in circumference, and Trisha had a long story about a butterfly which I knew she was making up as she went along. Kathleen listened to them gravely, only expressing a little worry that the spider might have been a black widow, which I assured her it was not, and nodding her head occasionally, with her eyes looking far away over the water. "It would be nice to think that the spider went home and told his family about you," she said to Chris. "Spiders don't have families," said Chris, "and anyway, he didn't know me."

"Spiders are ladies," said Trisha, "and they do have families, they have little girl spiders."

I thought that Kathleen looked at her oddly. "How do you know?" she asked, to which Trisha replied that I had told her so. And regarding Kathleen with serious, round eyes, she inquired:

"Are you a girl or a lady?"

What she meant was that she would like her in either case, but if she turned out to be a girl they'd have more fun playing together.

Kathleen seemed to hesitate a moment before replying. I had a feeling that she would have liked to say "a girl," as much for her own sake as Trisha's. "I don't know," she said at last, almost sorrowfully, I thought. "Well, anyway," said Chris, "I'd rather be a whale." And he jumped up and ran down to the water.

A moment later Trisha joined him, and they played at being whales, chasing each other through the shallows, splashing and shouting.

Kathleen watched them, her face expressionless, her body in harmonious repose. It was good to be out in the sun again, to smell the fresh salt smell of the sea and the dry, rotted smell of the sand, to listen to the roll of the surf breaking a little way out and the hiss and follow of the foam as it swept up the beach. "They are dear children," she said. "How pitiful that their mother is dead."

How pitiful . . . ! It sounded so much like Trina that I caught my breath. "You seem to know a lot about us," I said shakily, not looking at her.

But I could tell that she was smiling. "After all," she said, "you're well known around here. All I had to do was ask."

I looked at her then, but she was serene and kind, she wasn't laughing at me. "Well," I said more boldly, "how about you? I couldn't find out anything." "Nobody knows me," she said.

I thought I could at least get her to tell me where she lived, but she only shook her head.

"It's no use," she said; "you wouldn't know the place."

We talked about ordinary things—about the weather, and Chris's spider, and the life and death of the little sand crabs which Uncle Harry used for bait. "They cry when the hook goes into them," she said, "but nobody hears them, and they resign themselves to their fate, which is to be eaten very soon." "They must know they're going to be eaten," I said, "the first time they know what they are." "They never know what they are," she said. "They think they're beautiful."

A moment later she was laughing at Trisha who came out of the water dripping like a little spaniel, and ran up the sand to us and threw herself down on a towel. "Where are your fins?" she asked. "I don't see them anywhere."

Once again I thought the girl gave her an odd

look. "I didn't need them," she said, "so I left them at home."

It was a good day on the beach with Kathleen. I found her gay and quick, responsive to all the life about her, and gentle with the children. Her mind was crowded with unexpected bits of information, such as the travel habits of eels, and the making of bouillabaisse, and the sounds that crabs make when they talk to one another. It enchanted the children, and they spent several minutes with their heads under the water, saying cri-ik, cri-ik, and blowing air bubbles.

I couldn't get her to tell me anything about herself. She parried my questions lightly, but I felt that she was disturbed by them. I couldn't help being a little vexed at the mystery she made of herself. I thought the best thing to do was to ignore it.

We swam together while the children rested, walking down to the water side by side, my body so dark next to hers, and plunged through the first big wave together; and almost at once I missed her and didn't find her again until I had churned my way out beyond the breakers and was floating on my back in the long, easy swells. She came up to me with a curiously graceful, lazy motion, and we swam for a while side by side, I doing my usual crawl and throwing up geysers of spray with every beat, and she moving like an eel, with scarcely a ripple. Then she dived suddenly, and came up some distance away, and I swam over to her while she watched me with a kind of grave concern, and then we raced each other in to the beach, planing in on the breakers in a smother of foam.

We lay on the sand together to rest and catch

our breath, and I found myself looking at her and wondering. She lay there beside me, relaxed, breathing easily, her long hair, free of the kelp that had bound it, spread out over her shoulders, drying in the sun, and little drops of water still on her arms and legs. What do I know about her? I thought. She is well educated, I'm quite sure of that; she has probably taken a course in zoology somewhere, perhaps at the Marine Biological Laboratory in La Jolla or Woods Hole. She is traveled, because she knows that you can't make bouillabaisse without merlan, which is a fish found only in the waters off the south of France. And because she is gay and gentle with children, I imagine she was brought up in a convent, which would make her a Catholic—though she wears no medal around her neck. I think she is Irish, from her name, for all she says she's not; and she has either run away from a cruel stepfather, or her heart has been broken by an unhappy love affair. And she is the best swimmer I have ever seen.

The children and I had brought our lunch to the beach, and we shared it with Kathleen, who added to the usual peanut-butter sandwiches little fillets of raw fish, which she ate with lemon, and which were quite delicious. They seemed to be some kind of herring. After lunch the children lay down to nap in the sun, and Kathleen told them the story of Ysot of Brittany, who jumped into the sea for love of a shepherd, and was turned into a whelk; she remembered her father's palace with its hundred rooms, and built her own house of many chambers, each finer and more delicate than the one before. "I wouldn't want to be a whelk," said Trisha. "I wouldn't want to be anything except what I am." "The whelk," said Kathleen, "lives on oysters; it's a very rich life." "I don't want a rich life," said Trisha sleepily. "I'm only little."

And putting her face down on her hand, and closing her eyes, she added:

"It should have been a prince on a milk white steed."

Kathleen turned to me, quite mortified. "He should have been," she said, "shouldn't he?" " 'Build thee more stately mansions, O my soul,' " I said, and that made her laugh.

"Children are all the same," I said; "life is either all black or all white to them. You don't throw yourself into the sea and become a whelk for nothing." "Oh," she said, "but he was such a lovely shepherd."

I was right, I told myself, it was an unhappy love affair.

And I murmured—quite falsely, as a matter of fact—"I'm sorry."

If I had expected her to blush, or to look grateful, I was in for a disappointment. "Sorry for what?" she asked; and the surprise in her voice made it clear that she hadn't the faintest notion of what I was talking about. Well, I thought not without relief, it isn't that, anyway.

The children slept, and woke, and bathed again, and we lay and watched them, and swam too, as before, Kathleen easing herself along beside me; and then it was time to go home and start the children's supper. It had been a long, lazy day. I couldn't afford to be lazy, but I didn't regret it. We said good-bye to Kathleen, and she smiled up at us from the sand, and shook hands with the children, and we started back to the house. Half way up the hill we turned to wave at her, but she wasn't there. I caught a glimpse of her head far out in the water; she was moving with that effortless motion of hers, her long hair floating out behind her. "She's wearing her fins," said Trisha triumphantly.

I hadn't thought she had them with her. But it did seem to me that she was moving very fast, and I thought I saw one fin gleam for a moment in the sunlight as she dove.

I didn't see her come up again, but she was quite far out, and I might have missed her.

CHAPTER 5

It was Trisha's idea to invite Kathleen to a dinner party at our house. It was a great occasion, being Trisha's first dinner party, and we spent the whole day getting ready for it, driving to market in the morning and preparing our chicken paprika in the afternoon. Chicken paprika was what I cooked best, and we decided on fresh corn and gingerbread and ice cream. Trisha made the gingerbread, while Chris set out the forks and knives and our best plates, being very careful with them, and the good water glasses. I brought out the silver candlesticks for the table, and laid a fire in the fireplace, although the weather was too warm for it, but Trisha said it made the house look nicer, and I thought so too.

Trisha had gotten herself up in the blue denim dress that was too short for her, with a ribbon in her hair, and Chris had put on his long pants which were a little too tight, and his shirt with the French cuffs. At six o'clock I went in to dress, with the chicken, brown and savory, warming in the oven, and the smell of gingerbread in the house.

Kathleen came at dusk. She had coiled her hair into a pale, soft knot at the back of her head, and she wore a light green dress the color of the sea the way it is sometimes near the shore, or in the shallow estuaries. She stood in the doorway and looked at the room and at us. "I knew it would be like this," she said simply.

Chris went up to shake hands with her, bashful and awkward in his long trousers, and Trisha followed, smoothing down her little skirt, and tossing her head to show off her ribbon. Nobody said anything; and I asked Kathleen if she would like a drink. "Yes, please," she said.

I made two martinis, and we moved over to the window-seat to drink them. The children stood in front of us with solemn faces, and every now and then Chris would look down at the floor and move his feet a little, and Trisha would smooth her skirt and feel for the ribbon in her hair. "Well," I said, "skoal," and Kathleen said "skoal," and we smiled at each other.

"It was so nice of you to ask me to dinner," she said. I told her that it was Trisha's idea, and Trisha blushed and bridled with pride. "I made the dessert," she declared.

Chris came up to Kathleen and put his hand very gently on her hair. Then without a word he turned and bounded across the room, threw himself head down into a chair, and made violent swimming motions with his arms. After that he turned around and sat up very straight with his stubby legs stuck out in front of him, and looked at us stonily. I knew what the matter was: he felt that he had been left out of things.

"Chris set the table," I said, wanting to make it all right for him again. Kathleen glanced at the plates and glasses glinting in the firelight, and then she looked at Chris. "It's beautiful," she said. Chris didn't answer, he turned and looked up at the ceiling with an air of indifference, but I knew that he was ready to weep with delight and self-pity.

It took the children until the end of dinner to feel as free with Kathleen as they had on the beach. It took me almost as long. There is something fragrant and mysterious about a woman in her dresses; she is at the same time more desirable, and more vulnerable, delicious, fragile, and formidable.

Kathleen was good with the children. Trisha was solemn and full of manners, and Chris beamed and said nothing, and ate steadily. We all helped wash the dishes, and then it was time for the evening story, and after the story it was the children's bedtime. I asked Trisha if she'd like Kathleen to hear her prayers, and she said No, and so Chris said No, too. But she gave me a particularly hard hug afterwards, and I guessed that she would have liked Kathleen to have heard them after all, only she was too shy to say so. She and Chris God-blessed the usual people, myself, and Aunt Clara and Nana McHugh, and each other; and Trisha wished blessings on two little girls she'd met on the beach and whose names she didn't know. I was sure I heard Chris mutter Kathleen's name very fast at the end.

"Chris said a God-bless for you," I told her when I came out. She was silent for a moment, and then she said: "Poor little soul."

I didn't think Chris thought of himself as a poor little soul, and I told her so. "He was only three when his mother died," I said, "and he's almost six now. He lives in a man's world." She gave me a merry, mocking look. "A man's world?" she asked. "With Trisha in it?"

I had to laugh at that too. "Oh well," I said, "Trisha—" as though she was something altogether uncommon, and not to be counted in the ordinary run of things. It was a man's world, I meant, not counting Trisha.

But she was not to be put off so easily. "It may be a man's world," she said, "but it's run by women. By women's love," she added, still mocking me, I thought.

"Men have always had the great thoughts," I argued, "and the inventions." "True," she said; "and the great wars, too.

"But love is a woman's life. From the cradle to the grave . . . and beyond it."

When a man is alone with a woman, sooner or later they always speak of love, though it may not be for each other. Their pulses beat a little faster, and their glances become more thoughtful, and even tender; it might be you, their eyes say, or it might not; some day, perhaps, or never.

She wasn't mocking me now; and something in her voice—some note of sorrow, perhaps—stilled the light answer I might have made. I thought of the great love stories of the world; of *Jane Eyre,* of *The Red Lily,* of *Green Mansions* . . . it was true, it was the woman always whose love brought all about, and moved the mountains. It was the woman who was immortal, not the man. It was Juliet's story, not Romeo's; it is for Juliet that people weep and throw pennies into the well at Verona.

But if women moved mountains, they made the wars too, I thought, remembering Guinevere and Cleopatra, and that wife of Tiernan O'Ruairc, King of Breffny, who ran off with the King of

Leinster and brought the English into Ireland. "And what about Helen," I asked, "who brought about the ruin of Troy?" "It was only an excuse," she said. "What they wanted was gold." "Well, then," I said obstinately, "if women made no wars, there have been men who loved as well as any. What of Orpheus, who braved the underworld for his Euridyce?" "That one!" she said in scorn; "how well did he love? He had no faith at all, for he looked back and lost her." "What of the fisherman," I said, "who caught the little mermaid?"

I was smiling, but she was silent, looking out through the darkened window in which the lights of the room were dimly reflected against the pale night sky. "That is the saddest story of all," she said.

Below us the invisible sea grumbled in the dark.

ness; far off along the coast, lights twinkled above the water in the soft blue air of the summer night. It was beautiful and peaceful out there over the ocean. The stars hung bright and quiet in the sky; a coyote barked back in the hills, and then, suddenly, all the coyotes were singing. It wasn't barking or howling, and it didn't sound like animals at all, it was singing. There were many voices, and they rose and fell and wove themselves into curious harmonies, mournful and full of longing and strangely sweet. I didn't know whether Kathleen had ever heard them before, but I hadn't; they sang for quite a long time, and we sat there, and didn't say anything, and listened. And as I listened, I felt the night close in around me like a sea, full of secrets—the press and anguish of all those creatures, seen and unseen, whose bodies made up the tangible world in which I lived. I felt the emptiness of space above me and below me, the vast abyss with its stars and planets scattered there like pebbles—or like seeds flung from a sower's hand, to fall . . . where?

How lonely man is in the face of that immense emptiness, tied to his own momentary bones, unable to communicate with beast or bird, with flower or fly. How he reaches out, to talk to someone, or to God; and what a dusty answer he receives! Even the smallest mystery is beyond his understanding, the language of birds, the thoughts of beetles, the singing of coyotes in the hills at night. . . . And far out in space, across the endless dark, far out beyond the distant edge of our own universe with its uncounted starry lights, lie other galaxies greater still, with others still beyond them. How the heart longs to understand,

and, failing, turns in that empty silence to another heart for comfort . . . too often all too brief.

The last ululations died away in the hills, and Kathleen stirred, and drew her hand away which had lain in mine. "Why does it sound so sad?" she whispered. I told her that I didn't know. "It's beautiful," she said, "but so sorrowful. Is life so mournful, then?" "You have to make your peace with sorrow," I said. "I know," she said; "and with being alone, and with the empty sea." "I wasn't always alone," I said.

I thought of the years with Trina, of the problems we'd had, the happiness as well as the unhappiness . . . the gradual coming-together of our two separate, obstinate selves, and how we had made peace at last with marriage and with each other, and how none of it had been easy.

For marriage is more than love and less than love, and for what each one gets he gives up something of his own.

"Was it good for you," she asked, "when your wife was alive?" I told her that we'd made our peace together. "You must have loved her very much," she said. "Yes," I said.

She thought about it for a while. "They say that love is stronger than death," she said at last.

I shook my head. "It isn't so," I said bitterly. "Death is stronger. Death is the strongest thing there is."

Her eyes were strangely sad and gentle as she looked at me. "Is it, Lenny?" she asked. "Are you sure?"

CHAPTER 6

"THE next check" had come, and we took a day off and drove in to Los Angeles to do some shopping. There was the doll's house and a new dress for Trisha to be got, and Chris had been promised a rubber surfboard; and I needed to get some books for myself, and some records. There wasn't very much for me to do at night but read or listen to music, and dream . . . or think about things, or sometimes both together. Sometimes I thought about my next day's work, sketching out a chapter in my mind; sometimes I thought about the past; but most of the time I thought about Kathleen.

She hadn't been to the beach for over a week, and I hadn't heard from her at all. Even the children hadn't seen her, not anywhere. It shouldn't have bothered me, but it did; the fact was, I missed her. There was so much about her that I didn't understand; I kept telling myself that she didn't owe me any explanations, but the more I tried to put her out of my mind, the more I found myself thinking about her; and the more I thought, the more I wondered. I wondered why she wouldn't tell me who she was, and where she lived; and why she came and went the way she did. I remembered how she had appeared in the doorway the night of Trisha's dinner party, and none of us had seen her come; and how she had left, going down the hill to the beach instead of up to the road where people left their cars. I knew that she hadn't left her car there; I went up myself, to look for it.

As I say, I missed her. It took me a little while to realize that I was going to the beach each day simply in the hope of seeing her; and that I felt restless lying on the sand in the sun, because she wasn't there.

Where was she? I had no idea. She might have been in China, for all I knew; she made such a secret of herself. But what could a young girl like that have to conceal? Why should she want to hide? I couldn't figure it out; I had no answer to it at all.

Neither had Dick Basset, who was eating his lunch at Scandia when we got there. I ordered a bouillabaisse for the three of us, and went over to his table to speak to him. He was with a young woman whom he introduced as Alice, and whose last name I immediately forgot as I always do—if, in fact, I ever heard it at all. Alice was an actress; she had had a small part in one of Dick's television stories, and looked forward to another. She was an amiable young creature, eagerly alive, and obviously expected great things from the world. At the same time, she was a realist and knew that there was no reason to believe that they would come to her without luck, persistence, and the help of astrology. She was a Virgo, and each morning she studied the astrological chart in the *Los Angeles Times,* to judge her chances for the day. "It's kind of general," she explained, "but sometimes they tell you something important. Like the time it said 'good for making contacts,' and I met Dick about a week later." What she looked forward to was success, and having her own astrologer to read the stars for her every day.

"The trouble with you," Dick said when I told him about Kathleen, "is that you don't see enough people. You sit out there on the beach with the sea-gulls, and you get dreams in your hair. You say this girl won't tell you where she lives, or how to find her? She's playing some kind of game with you, that's all—some kind of foggy game." "It's damp by the sea," said Alice. "I lived there one year, and I know."

As Uncle Harry would have said, Dick had the word. "She's trying to make herself interesting to you," he said; "she's trying to rouse your interest.

I don't believe her name is Kathleen at all She simply took it out of the Irish Anthology.

He waggled a finger at me solemnly. "That's only in the first place," he said. "In the second place, she hides her car down the road a ways, and comes in over the sand like a crab. Is she a crab?" "No," I said. "Well, then," said Dick, "has she got whiskers? If she's got whiskers, she's a seal." "I knew a seal once," said Alice, "down at La Jolla."

"She's not a seal," I said, "and she's not a crab. She's a girl. A very nice-looking girl, as a matter of fact. She wears seaweed in her hair, and she swims like an eel." "She couldn't be an eel," said Alice positively.

"You know what I think?" said Dick. "I think you made her up." But I knew he didn't think so, and I guessed he was a little surprised. I hadn't cared one way or another about anybody since Trina's death, and there I was, talking about a girl I'd scarcely met, as though it mattered. He sat there, studying me, and I thought that he was worried.

"Maybe I'd better come down one of these days," he said at last, "and look her over." "Suppose I can't find her?" I asked. "You'll find her," said Alice. "We'll help you look."

So it was arranged that Dick and Alice would come down some day for a beach picnic. It might be fun at that, I thought; and I could do with a little fun.

Alice wanted to know what month I was born, and I told her January. "You're a Capricorn," she said; "that's very interesting. A Capricorn has Power, only you've got to be careful not to be stubborn. You've got Imagination in your sign, too. Let me see your hand."

I held out my hand and she took it in both of hers, turning it this way and that to catch the light. Her fingers were soft and warm, not cool like Kathleen's, and I could see Dick watching her. She studied the lines of my palm, and measured my fingers one against the other. "Yes," she said, "you've got Imagination. And you don't fall in love easily. I mean . . . if you like somebody, you're—you know—faithful."

I thought she gave Dick a quick, almost shy look, before she turned back to me again. "What do you do?" she asked. "I mean, what do you do for a living?"

Dick told her that I wrote children's stories. "I love children's stories," she said. "They have such happy endings." "Mine are about pirates," I said, "and sea-witches." "That's what I mean," she said; "you've got Power."

I took the children to Hunter's Book Store in Beverly Hills to get the books, and downtown to the Gateway To Music for the records. I got a fine old recording of Stracciari, who was a great singer before I was born. How beautifully they used to sing in the old days; silver and gold those voices of the past, honey and velvet. They always make me think of gaslight and snow, of women's furs, and carriages, of violets, and far-off, muted love affairs. Music isn't what it was; and according to Uncle Harry Cole, women's furs aren't as fragrant as they used to be.

Trisha got her dress, posturing self-consciously in front of the dress-shop mirror, and Chris got his surfboard, and we started home. It had been a good day as far as getting things done was concerned, but I had an uneasy feeling about it, just the same. I had a feeling that something was wrong; I kept thinking that I shouldn't have talked about Kathleen the way I had, that she wouldn't have liked it. I tried to remember what I had said. . . . It was Dick who had called her a seal, not I. She was just a girl I'd met on the beach, and I couldn't see why I should worry about it.

But I did; and the worst of it was that I didn't know what I was worried about. I only knew that I had come to count on her being there, to being with her, and that she wasn't there.

Trisha must have sensed the way I felt, or else she felt the same way, for she pushed herself up close to me and put her hand out to pat my arm.

"Won't Kathleen be surprised," she said, "when she sees my new dress?" "Yes," I said; "I'm sure she will."

"I'll wear it to supper," said Trisha, "and I'll wear it when we go to her house." "She hasn't asked us," I said, "and besides, we don't know where it is."

She didn't say anything for a moment, looking out of the window at the houses as we went down San Vicente. "It's a fairy house," she said at last dreamily, "and it's in the middle of the ocean. It's full of emeralds and pearls and rosy coral, and little tiny sea-horses." "Then maybe she won't come back at all," I said, "if that's where she lives."

Chris was trying to blow up his surfboard in the back seat. "Maybe she went to China," he said cheerfully. "Maybe she swam there." "That's a long swim," I said; "China is a long way off." "I can swim fifty strokes," said Chris, "and she can swim better."

"Anyway," said Trisha, "she wouldn't go away without saying good-bye." She seemed quite positive about it. "I hope she won't," I said, smiling down at her.

It was good to come out onto the shore road again and breathe the clean air of the sea. The road went along the water, and past the little houses of Malibu, and then up above the sea, and we could look down at it and see it shining in the sun all the way to the horizon. "There's China over there," said Chris, pointing to the dim blue loom of Catalina in the south.

The sun was half way down the sky when we got home, and the shadows were long and slanting. The house had an empty look, and my heart sank. I hadn't expected anything else, but I was disappointed anyway—just as I always was. In the old days I'd come home and there'd be Trina in the kitchen, and the children with her, and a good smell of cooking in the air. An empty house is a cold thing to come home to.

There was a package at the door; I didn't see it at first, until Trisha pointed it out to me. It was wrapped in some kind of green cloth, smooth and cold to the touch, and it was tied with a piece of sea-rotted rope festooned with mussels and seaweed. It looked like the sort of package a child would leave on the doorstep for another child. I told Trisha to open it.

Inside was a branch of rosy coral, like the branch of a living tree.

We took it in and put it on the mantle over the fireplace, and it caught the light from the window and glowed like a peach tree in bloom. "Kathleen was here," said Trisha. "She left it for us."

I knew it was from Kathleen, too, it couldn't have been from anyone else. And suddenly everything was all right again.

CHAPTER 7

SHE hadn't left us; she hadn't gone to China, or to her fairy home under the sea with its pearls and its emeralds and its sea-horses. Though I sometimes wondered, those next few days, looking at the coral branch glowing on the mantlepiece, where she had got it. She hadn't found it skin-diving off Malibu. And while I didn't know very much about coral, I thought it would have been an expensive thing to buy.

So once again it was necessary to thank her, and still she kept herself out of sight. I couldn't understand it, I couldn't think of any reason for it, and as the days went by without her coming to the beach, without my seeing her at all, I began to get a little angry. What was it Dick had said about a foggy game? It seemed to me that I was being made part of a very foggy game indeed . . . but for what reason, or to what purpose? Was she trying—as Dick said—to "interest" me? to make me think more of her? If so, she was going about it in a very childish way.

Or did she—and I had to admit that the thought troubled me—want me to think less?

Old Uncle Harry Cole came climbing up the hill one day to share my luncheon with me. He brought me a bass, not a very big one, but enough for the children's supper. "How are things with you, Lenny?" he inquired. "You getting on with your book?"

I told him that the book was going slowly. "That's too bad," he said. "You ever find that girl you were looking for?"

I told him that I'd found her, and that I'd lost her again. "Well, now," he said, "I like to think that nothing's ever lost in the world. I'm glad you found her, it relieves my mind."

I made a face that Trisha calls my mumpish face. "The dinosaurs were lost," I said, "a hundred million years ago." "Well, yes," he admitted, "you can say that, seeing no one remembers them. Maybe what I meant was, nothing is lost so long as somebody remembers it."

I remember Trina, I thought; and she is lost.

"You got a little beer?" asked Uncle Harry, "to go with these sandwiches?"

We took our beer and our sandwiches and went out to sit on the doorstep in the sun. "If I only knew why," I said. "If there was some reason for it. It's making such a mystery of herself that I don't understand."

Uncle Harry Cole put his hand on my shoulder in a fatherly way. "Lenny," he said earnestly, "you don't want to let yourself be upset because there are things you don't understand. Every one of us is a mystery to every other living creature. I had a wife once thought me scarcely worth talking about, and no bigger than a grunion. But to that same grunion, flopping on the sand, time I caught him and popped him into a pail, I was big as death and twice as ugly. They were both right in their way."

"I don't know what you were to your wife," I said, "but you were death to the grunion."

"They neither of them knew me for what I was," said Uncle Harry. "I was a mystery to them. That grunion was only doing what nature intended, and I interfered with him. You know what a mystery is? It's something you haven't got the word for. That wife of mine didn't have the right word for me. The way she saw me, I was a grunion."

He took a long pull on his beer, and wiped his lips with the back of his hand. "You take an ant," he said. "You got the word for an ant?"

"No," I said.

"Nor he for you," said Uncle Harry. "You're a pure mystery to him; you're just a power of nature, a striding nightmare like the Johnstown Flood. She's probably home with a cold."

"Who is?" I asked.

"This girl of yours," he said. "Kathleen."

"How did you know her name?" I asked.

"Hell," he said; "you told me."

A few days later I got a telephone call from Dick Basset. He wanted to talk to me about an old story of mine that had appeared in the *Post* three or four years back. He'd been at a party with a Mr. Goldberg who was a producer at Universal, and Mr. Goldberg had read my story when it first came out and had never forgotten it. "He thinks it might make a picture," Dick said, "and he wants to talk to you." "You mean he wants to buy it?" I asked; and my voice squeaked a little. "That depends," said Dick. "How about coming in on Friday, and we'll have lunch and go over to Universal together?" "Fine," I said; "I'll be there. What did you say his name was?"

"Goldberg," said Dick. "I'll tell him you're coming."

I wrote Mr. Goldberg's name down, so as not to forget it; and then I set about looking for a baby-sitter for the children.

When Trisha heard that I wanted to hire someone to sit with them for a day, she approached me with a serious air. "It's silly to pay somebody to look after us," she said, "when I can do it just as good myself." I pointed out to her that she was hardly grown-up enough, but she waved it aside as irrelevant. "I'm grown-up enough to look after Chris," she said, "and I can help him look after me. And we won't go anywhere, not down to the beach or anything, and I won't let him play with matches, and we can have shredded wheat for lunch and bread-and-sugar and things. And you'll be home in time for supper, and anyway, I could put Chris to bed if I had to." "He'd never let you," I said. "I know," she admitted; "but maybe he would if I hit him."

"Well, thank you very much," I said, "but I think I'll look for a baby-sitter just the same." "I wish you wouldn't call it that," said Trisha. "Couldn't you call it something older?"

She went away, but presently she was back again, in a business-like way. "How much do you have to pay them?" she asked; "for staying with us?" "Oh, about three or four dollars," I said.

I could see that she was turning something over in her mind. "I'd do it for twenty-five cents," she said at last, and gave me a hopeful look.

As it turned out, I couldn't find anyone after all, and so Trisha got her twenty-five cents—in advance, which was what she held out for. It seemed little enough, when I thought of all the money I was going to make if Mr. Goldberg bought my story. "Will we be rich?" she asked, and I said Yes, I thought so. "Then I can get a turtle," said Chris.

I thought Trisha looked a little flushed on Friday morning, but I put it down to excitement. I was pretty excited myself, by that time; it isn't often a writer gets a chance to sell a story to pictures. I asked Trisha what tie I ought to wear, and I let her pick it out for me; I don't usually wear a tie, but I wanted to make a good impression. I went over everything with the children again, and they promised to stay indoors or in the yard, not to go to the beach, and to eat a sensible luncheon. They were sensible children, and they knew how to take care of themselves. Just as long as they stayed off the road, and didn't play with matches or go near the water . . .

I started off down the coast highway in the morning sunshine, and everything felt good. I was a successful writer, on my way to sell a story to a motion picture studio. I wondered how much I'd get: ten thousand, fifteen? I thought of all the things we could do with so much money; I could invest it, I could buy a house, I could put braces on Trisha's teeth, I could put it into life insurance . . . I could stop writing children's stories for a while. . . . I felt big, and full of breath, like Trisha's blowfish.

I went down past Zuma and Paradise Cove and crossed to the Valley through Topanga Canyon, and met Dick at the Sportsmen's Lodge, and he took me to Universal. The girl at Reception kept us waiting a while, and then we were told to go to Bungalow Seven, on the lot.

I hadn't forgotten Mr. Goldberg's name, but it

didn't matter, because he and Dick did most of the talking. He remembered my story, and he wanted to buy it and have Dick do the adaptation; but it wasn't for the studio, it was for himself. What he had in mind was something for television. He wanted an option on the story, until he could find out what to do with it.

He was a small, sharp man; he had been a song writer in Tin Pan Alley, and he had made a picture called *Hot Cake* that had cost the studio two hundred and seventy thousand dollars and had grossed a million five. He explained the reason for his success:

"The gimmick," he said, "is this: *Hot Cake* was a television show. So we covered costs to begin with. It looked good upstairs, and we had something to take around. What's more, looking at it ourselves that way, we could tell what it needed.

We paid the writer—the fellow who wrote the original story—for a half hour television show, so that didn't cost us too much. The fellow who wrote the script took a percentage of the profits on the film, and he came up with a nice little piece of money, and everybody was happy."

He and Dick discussed some changes he wanted made, while I sat there and looked out of the window; "First of all," he said, "we've got to make the woman a little younger, and the man a little older. Because nobody is big at the box office any more, under forty. So the man is forty, which means if he is fifty in real life he is still good in the part. The woman is maybe twenty-two or three, which they all look like, anyway.

"And in the second place," he said, "we want an up-beat ending. You know . . . with heart."

"What will that do to my story?" I asked.

He looked at me in surprise. "Why should it do anything?" he said.

My story was a love story, but it was about young people, and it didn't have an up-beat ending. "What I wrote," I said, "was real. It was about real people. To me it had heart."

"Sure," said Mr. Goldberg: "heart—like you say it. But what I mean is heart like I say it. Your story is about real people? All right, I understand that. But Lenny, listen Baby: what do real people do? They make love, and they have trouble. In show business, you do not leave people with trouble; they would not watch the screen any more, they would turn the set off. We are only here to make money, not to write philosophies."

"It's like I told you, Lenny," said Dick: "the glory has departed."

"Glory never had it so good," said Mr. Goldberg simply. "We got sixty million people watching television every night."

He wanted to pay me a hundred dollars out of his own pocket for a six months' option, and then fifteen hundred and a percentage. Dick managed to get me two hundred to begin with and twenty-five hundred if he took up the option; and after that we went back to the Sportsmen's Lodge where I'd left my car. We neither of us said much, there wasn't much to say. It was all pretty disappointing, considering what I'd expected. "How about a drink?" said Dick. "One for the road."

We went in and sat at the bar, and the drinks made me feel better. After the second or third, I started to tell Dick about the blowfish. "There's this fish," I said, "that blows himself up with air, to make himself feel big. But all it is, is air. Phtt! he's back to nothing again." " 'The glory that was

Greece,' " said Dick, " 'and the grandeur that was Rome.' " "The grandeur that was M.G.M.," I said, "the way you tell it." "It was there," said Dick dreamily. "It was there like the smell of honeysuckle, all around me." "That's a lovely smell, honeysuckle," I said.

We sat and looked at our drinks for a while, and then we finished them and ordered some more. "After all, Lenny," said Dick, "it could be a lot worse. Two hundred for an option isn't so bad." "It isn't that," I said; "it's how they make you feel." "I know," said Dick; "glory is when they do not turn the set off."

I laughed a little, because by this time it didn't matter so much any more. "I was going to buy a house," I said. "Can you imagine that!" "Sure," said Dick: "what price the great American dream?"

"About this blowfish," I said: "he puffs himself up with air, and then they unpuff him." "Who unpuffs him?" asked Dick. "Bring on the bastards." "No bastards," I said carefully; "it's a sea-witch does it. She's a friend of my daughter." "That's right," said Dick, "you've got a daughter." And gazing hazily up at the ceiling, he intoned: " 'Thy hyacinth hair, thy classic face, Thy Naiad arms have brought me home.' " "You just reminded me," I said. "It's time I went home."

I leaned across the bar and beckoned to the bartender. "Another round," I said. "Make it two," said Dick. "One for the road, and one for my baby." "Don't forget Baby," I said. "One for Baby."

I knew I was drunk even before I got into my car, but it all felt good, and all of a sudden two hundred dollars seemed like a fortune. There was a lot of traffic on Ventura, but not much in the Canyon, and I didn't have any trouble till I got near the coast highway, and then I hit a heavy fog, a real pea-souper. I drove very slowly, but a lot of the time I didn't know which side of the road I was on. Once or twice I stopped altogether, and just sat there, listening, and peering out at the fog. Cars would go by, their lamps looming up like yellow blurs, and they'd pass me slowly, feeling their way like blind things. I could make out a few dim house lights here and there, but I didn't know where I was, and I didn't see how I'd know my own house when I came to it. I was cold, and I had to clench my teeth to keep from shivering, and I kept taking long, deep breaths trying to sober up.

I was beginning to feel worried, too, and I felt lonely, more lonely than I had ever felt before.

Fog is a creature from the sea, it has its own life and venom, and it has an enmity for the land and land creatures. It creeps between them and the land they know, it saps their warmth and the help they are to one another. A man is all alone in a fog, without friends or landmarks; whatever he turns to, withdraws, becomes insubstantial and fades from sight. A man was made to live in the bright land, in plain view, not in the sea, or in yesterday.

A car came out of the fog at me, blaring its horn, and swerved sharply, and missed me; and with a lurch of fear I realized that I was on the wrong side of the road. I pulled the car over to the right, and stopped it, and sat there with my hands on the wheel, and I thought, This is as far as I can go; I mustn't try to go any farther.

I must have been more drunk than I thought,

because after a while the car was moving again, and Trina was driving. At least, I thought it was Trina. "I didn't get the house, Trina," I said, "or the life insurance. I got a pair of pants for Chris." "He'll need suspenders, then," she said. "Red flannel ones," I said, "with bits of string."

But was it Trina, or was it Kathleen there beside me? It was Kathleen; I could see the pale, witch-cloud of her hair. Yet it was Trina's voice. "You're late," she said. "I must get you home."

I felt as though I wanted to cry; and at the same time I felt a great comfort, as though everything was the way it used to be. "I was all alone," I said. "Where did you come from?" "It's no use," she answered; "you wouldn't know the place."

And then suddenly I was driving again, and I was by myself, and there was no more fog, and there was Paradise Cove and Trancas, and then the house was there in front of me with its windows lighted in the dusk, and the sky behind it green with evening. It looked warm and homely, with smoke coming out of the chimney; someone had lit a fire, and I thought the children shouldn't have done that, they promised not to.

When I got to the door, Chris opened it, and threw his arms around my knees. "Trisha's sick," he said. "And Kathleen's here."

CHAPTER 8

She stood slender and tall and shadowy at the door of Trisha's room, and I thought I had never been more glad to see anyone. Through the doorway I could see Trisha propped up in bed, looking small, and shadowy too. Kathleen moved out of the way, and I went in and looked down at my daughter. I felt her forehead; it was hot and damp, and her eyes were heavy. "How do you feel?" I asked, and she shook her head. "You shouldn't have gone to the beach," I told her. "I didn't," she said.

And lifting her hand to mine, she whispered:

"Mommy was here."

I turned to look at Kathleen, but she had left the room. "I'm going to take your temperature," I said.

I wasn't ready to think about Trina then. We had both of us seen her, and Trina was dead; you don't see dead people. Maybe some day I'd think about it, but not then.

Trisha's temperature was 103. "I'm going to call the doctor," I said.

She shook her head again, wearily. "I had the doctors," she said, "and one of them gave me a sea-horse."

I looked over at her bedside table, and there was a little sea-horse swimming around in a bowl of water. "That was nice of him," I said. "Who told him to come?" "Mommy did," she said.

Chris came in quietly, and sat down next to the bed; and I went out and closed the door. I found Kathleen standing in front of the fireplace with her back to the fire. "Was the doctor here?" I asked. She told me he'd come, and that there was nothing to worry about. "It's just a cold," she said; "the fever won't last more than a day. Keep her in bed, he said, and keep her warm, and feed her fruit juice and lots of water."

I didn't realize how worried I'd been until then. "How did it happen?" I asked. "I mean . . . how did you happen to be here?" "I heard her crying," she said.

She must have been passing along the beach, I

thought, below the house; and that's how she heard her. But it wasn't like Trisha to cry. "She said there were two doctors," I declared. "Was she dreaming?" "No," said Kathleen; "I sent for mine first, he's nearer." "And then?" I asked. "Then I found your doctor's name," she said, "and I called him, and he came and said not to worry." "What did your doctor say?" I asked. She looked at me quietly. "He said what a sweet child," she declared.

"Was that all?"

"Yes," she said.

It sounded strange, but everything was strange, as though it was happening far away, or under water. I wondered if I had a fever, too. "Did he give her a sea-horse?" I asked. "He always does," she said.

And she added in a matter-of-fact way:

"I have some supper for you."

We sat across from each other at the little table in front of the fire, where Trisha had had her party, and we ate together. She had cooked me a chowder, but she must have brought it from her own house, because she ladled it out of a big abalone shell, and there were a lot of things in it I didn't recognize. "It's funny," I said: "I keep having to thank you. It's almost as though you kept watch over us." "Somebody has to," she said lightly, but her eyes were grave.

After a while I said: "I've missed you, Kathleen."

She told me that she'd stayed away to let me get on with my work. "It wasn't a good idea," I said. I told her that I hadn't been able to write at all. "Is it my fault?" she asked. "Yes," I said.

We stared at each other, and she got up and

came around the table and bent down and kissed me. "I didn't know I had to watch over you, too," she said.

Her hair brushed my cheek for a moment, and she went back to her seat again. "Is that better?" she asked.

"Yes," I said. But the strange thing was, it wasn't better, it was worse. That first kiss should have been like dew and wonder and the whole wide world, and both of us should have been on tiptoe and shining; but it wasn't like that, it made me feel sad.

She must have known how I felt, because when I looked across at her there was a puzzled, hurt look on her face. "I'll get you some coffee," she said.

She went into the kitchen, and brought back the coffee and the two cups. "Was there much fog along the coast," she asked politely, "as you came through?"

I couldn't look at her. "Why do you ask me that?" I said. "You know there was, don't you?"

When she didn't answer, I glanced up; she was looking at me in an odd way, almost regretfully, I thought. "You were there, weren't you?" I asked.

She let her breath out in a faint sigh. It was as though she'd come to a place she'd somehow hoped she'd never come to. "I don't know what you mean, Lenny," she said quietly. "How could I have been?"

How indeed? Yet someone had been with me out there in the fog; someone had been beside me in the car; I had seen her and talked to her. "I don't know," I said wearily. "I wish I did." "I was with the children," she said.

Her eyes held mine steadily, and I knew that she was begging me to believe her, and that I had to believe her because if I didn't there wouldn't ever be anything else for us. I felt very tired, as though I'd been far out on a dark sea, and had come back again. "I guess I was out over my depth," I said; "I was way far out."

She sighed again, with relief, and I knew that the moment of danger for both of us was over. "People shouldn't go too far out," she said.

That was what Trina used to say; I almost expected to hear Dick tell me that my wife was a wise woman. But it wasn't Trina, it was Kathleen; and I didn't know which of them I loved.

She made no move to come close to me again. We sat by the fire, and talked; she told me what to feed sea-horses, and I told her about Mr. Goldberg, and how, for Dick Basset, the glory was departed. "The world has changed for writers," I declared. "It doesn't smell like honeysuckle any more." "Perhaps it will change back again," she said. "No," I said; "we've all been drowned like lost Atlantis. 'Full fathom five thy father lies; Of his bones are coral made . . .' I never thanked you for the coral," I said. "Trisha did," she said.

We were polite and a little wary with each other. I told her about Dick and Alice, and how they were planning to come down to help me look for her. "I told them I couldn't find you," I said, "and they said they'd come and help me look." "That was very kind of them," she remarked. "Is that her name—? Alice?" "She's quite nice, really," I declared. "She believes in astrology." "Oh?" said Kathleen.

She expressed some curiosity about the book I was writing, and I went to my desk and took out the manuscript. "It's about a sea-witch," I said; and I added apologetically, "I don't know much about her." "But Trisha does," she said; "doesn't she?" "Yes," I said, "Trisha does."

She asked me to read some of it to her, and so I read her the opening paragraph:

" 'The sea-witch came in on the tide, riding on the waves like foam, and her hair floated out behind her like seaweed. She came to the beach and lay there breathing slightly, and her eyes searched everywhere like a hungry gull. And Michael Doyle's little daughter Vicky, walking along the beach in search of colored shells . . .' " "That would be the Caribbean," said Kathleen.

She was leaning forward in her chair, listening intently. "I've never been to the Caribbean," I said awkwardly. "It doesn't matter," she said; "I can tell you about it." And like a child, she added:

"Go on."

But I felt self-conscious, and I went back to my desk and put the manuscript away. "I haven't been able to go on with it," I said.

She didn't say anything for a while. "What do the children think of it?" she asked at last. I told her that Chris preferred stories about pirates, and that Trisha and I hadn't been able to agree about the witch. "She doesn't want her to be ugly," I said. "And did you make her ugly?" she asked. "I did," I replied: "ugly and hungry, but now I don't know."

I gave an awkward laugh. "Anyway," I said, "Trisha says if she's hungry she ought to have plenty of peanut butter and spinach." But Kathleen didn't see anything to laugh at. "Spinach?" she asked. "No decent sea-witch would bother with it." "That's what I told her," I declared; and I added innocently:

"What was in the chowder?"

She shrugged her shoulders. "Oh," she said carelessly, "bits of this and that."

She was thinking about something else; she sat staring into the fire, with her chin cupped in her hand. "So it's my fault you haven't got on with it," she said at length.

"My heart isn't in it any more," I said. She seemed to know what I meant, because she nodded her head. "The daemon has gone out of you?" she asked. "Yes," I said.

"The children love you," she said gently; "isn't that a joy to you?" "Yes," I said; "but it isn't wonder. Love is wonder, Kathleen, as well as joy. Wonder, and benediction. That's all lost to me now."

She was silent for a long time, and when she spoke at last her voice was unsteady. "How do you know?" she asked. And then she did what Trina always did: she put up her hand the way Trina used to, with the palm up, and touched my cheek.

I leaned my head against her shoulder and closed my eyes. Her hair was cool and soft and smelled sweet and fresh and of the sea. "Love is never lost," she said. "It follows you, and finds you."

"I read a poem once," I said; "I remember the last lines of it. 'Beauty is only altered, never lost, And love, before the cold, November rain, Will make it's summer in the heart again.' I wish I believed it."

She laughed a little shakily "I think I'll get you some hot milk," she said, "and put you to bed." "Like the children?" I asked. "Why not?" she said. "Families need a daemon, too."

I took her hand and held it against my face. "I wish you didn't have to leave," I said.

There was a little pause, and then she said quite simply: "I don't have to."

When I woke the next morning, the sun was already glinting on the sea. Kathleen was gone; and so was Chris.

CHAPTER 9

THERE was a pot of coffee on the stove, and next to it a note from Kathleen, in spidery handwriting. *There was octopus in the chowder*, it said, *and deep-sea clams and lobster tails and prawns and merlan. If you have a headache, take two empirin. Trisha's temperature is down, but she ought to stay in bed another day. I gave her breakfast.*

KATHLEEN.

Don't worry about Chris. I'll take good care of him.

Trisha was sitting up in bed, looking bright and rosy when I peered in at her. Her face fell when I told her she'd have to stay in bed, but I brought her a pad and some colored pencils and her paper dolls, and after a while she resigned herself to her fate and began cutting out wardrobes. If she at all remembered thinking she had seen her mother, she didn't say so. "It's nice having Kathleen here," she said. "She cooked me an egg."

I went into my study and sat at my desk and stared through the window at the sea lying out there with summer on it. I didn't know what I felt; I didn't know whether to be happy or frightened. I wasn't so young any more, and I had two children and very little money; and whatever it was with Kathleen, it had gone beyond wishing and dreaming.

But what was it—actually? I didn't know. So often a girl's will is like a boy's will—and that's the wind's will, summer-short and ocean-airy. A summer thing, I thought; and with this girl of all others, about whom I could find out nothing, who seemed to come from the sea itself . . .

I thought: This isn't real. This isn't her real life, this sun and sand and sea, these summery nights. . . . In the fall she'll go back to her own, to her family, to her life in some city . . . I thought of her family. What use would they have for me? And this escapade, this romance of a young girl and a widower with two children . . .

Unless, of course . . .

Unless there was no family. Unless there was only Kathleen and myself. And—somehow—Trina.

Out there in the car, in the fog, I'd almost thought for a moment . . . but I'd been drunk, hadn't I? A drunken man could think he saw all kinds of things, couldn't he? He could even imagine . . .

Or could he?

I tried to remember everything that had happened, what I had said, what she had said, but it was all hazy in my mind. Had I fallen asleep in her arms? I didn't know. I remembered only the fragrance of her hair, and a tide of darkness flowing over me; and then waking in the morning alone.

Perhaps, I thought, when I see her again, I'll know. But then I thought—know what? And did I want to know?

They came back at noon, lugging a big fish up the hill with them, with sea-water all over them, and both of them laughing. "We went way out," said Chris, his eyes shining, "and Kathleen got him with a spear. Whoom!" "Way out?" I asked in surprise. "Sure," said Chris proudly, but I thought that he sounded a little surprised; "we must have swum half way to China."

I felt a moment's fright. "You had no business going out so far," I said—too sharply, and too quickly. He hung his head, and his lip trembled, and he moved closer to Kathleen and took her hand. "She said it was all right," he mumbled.

"I had him with me," Kathleen said simply, as though that explained everything. I turned away, feeling ashamed of myself, and a little foolish. What's done is done, I thought; and I thought he probably went out on his rubber surfboard, and he was safe enough anyway.

Besides, he was back again and so was she.

They must have been a long way out, I thought, to get a fish like that.

Kathleen took Trisha's lunch in to her on a tray, and I could hear them gossiping together, and Trisha's merriment at something Kathleen must have told her. I found that I was feeling sorry for myself, for being so left out of everything, the morning's fishing and the merriment, and I thought to myself, Whose friend is she after all, theirs or mine? And then I remembered how she had said that a family needed someone, too, to look after it, and I felt better, and took out my manuscript and began to work.

The work went along better, too, with the sound of Kathleen in the house and in the kitchen, and pans rattling, and things getting done. I could draw my own silence down around me, and be warm and comfortable in it, because of the good sounds in the house.

I was writing about Ys, the westernmost city, the City of Death, the key to the underworld or to the sea, where the sea-witch used to be at home; and as I wrote, the twilight world of the past closed in on me again as it used to do, and the unknown mysteries sounded their ocean-whisper in my ears. Where was Atlantis now, ruled by its ten divine and gentle kings? And where was Ys?

"Only the witch knew that," I wrote, "as she headed for the steep valleys of the far Atlantic where the great sea-monsters dwelt. Her sea-horses galloped before her, their tails streaming in the tides . . ."

I crossed out "the tides," and went into Trisha's room to see what a sea-horse looked like. It didn't look as though it could gallop very much.

Kathleen seemed to know where everything was in the house without my telling her. She cleaned the fish she'd caught, and sent Chris to a neighbor's to borrow some parsley; I offered to let her take my car to Trancas to do the marketing, but she seemed shy about it, and I had an idea that she didn't know how to drive.

As she worked she sang to herself, curious little melodies and snatches of songs none of which I'd ever heard before. Sometimes they sounded the way I imagined the Sirens must have sounded, and sometimes like old sea-chanteys, but the words —if there were words—were all in a foreign tongue, some language I didn't know. When I asked her what it was, she gave me a demure look. "You ought to know," she said, "writing about sea-witches." "Why?" I asked; "after all, I'm no authority." She straightened up at that, and tossed her head. "Oh," she said; "am I?" "I don't know," I said helplessly; "are you?" But she only laughed.

In the afternoon Uncle Harry Cole came up the hill to see me. He had Chris's rubber surfboard with him; it had a hole in one corner as big as a silver dollar, and was as limp as kelp. "Isn't this your boy's?" he asked, holding it out to me. "Yes," I said. "He was out on it this morning, a long way out. He must have torn it coming in; but he didn't tell me." "It's not strange he didn't tell you," said Uncle Harry, "seeing's I found it on the beach yesterday afternoon, and had it up to the house with me ever since."

We looked at each other for a moment, and then I shrugged my shoulders. "Well," I said easily, "in that case I guess he wasn't out on it after all." "Did he say he was?" asked Uncle Harry curiously. "No," I said. "Not on that, he wasn't," said Uncle Harry.

I had no time to think about it, because just then Kathleen came in from the kitchen. She seemed taken aback at finding Uncle Harry there, and hesitated in the doorway, half in and half out. "I've heard a lot about you from Lenny here," said Uncle Harry.

"Thank you," said Kathleen. "I've heard of you, too." But she didn't stay long, and very soon found an excuse to leave. "She's a queer girl," I said. "She's shy with strangers." "You take my advice," said Uncle Harry, "you'll throw her back into the sea again."

I thought he was joking, but he wasn't. "Lenny," he said, "I'm an old man, and I've seen stranger things come out of the water than this girl. But just the same—throw her back in. Take my word for it—that'll be the wisest thing you can do."

"She didn't come out of the sea," I said shortly. "Hell, I know that," said Uncle Harry; "what I'm trying to tell you is, she's not for you." "She's a lovely girl," I said, "and she's lovely with the children." "She'll never belong to you, Lenny," said Uncle Harry seriously, "and you might just as well know it."

I did know it, but I'd already made my peace with it, or thought I had. "All right," I said; "suppose it's only for a summer?" "A summer? Hell," said Uncle Harry; "you'll be eating your heart for Thanksgiving." "It's my heart," I said.

Trisha was allowed up for supper, and wanted to put on her new dress for the occasion, but Kathleen thought it too festive, and so did I. Still, Kathleen was a woman and therefore commanded Trisha's respect, which I did not, being a man, and arbitrary. Not that she gave in at once or without a struggle, even to Kathleen, but it was no more than half-hearted. "In my new dress," she said, "I'd feel healthier." "I know," said Kathleen, "but once you've had it on, it won't be new any more.

"Some day," said Kathleen, "there'll be a great occasion, and you'll wear it, and look beautiful." "Will I?" asked Trisha with a startled look.

She cheered up a good deal after that. "I didn't mind being sick," she said, "and I love my little sea-horse. I'm going to call him Henry. I'm going to take him swimming in my bath tub; I think he'll probably like that." "He'll die in a bath tub," I said; "he won't like it at all." "He won't die," said Trisha. "He loves me."

How sure she was of love, and how willing to offer it! But she knew when to step aside; and seeing, even before I did, how it was with Kathleen and me, she gave me up, at least for the time being. She gave me to Kathleen without regret—in fact, with what I imagine must have been relief that someone had come at last to help her carry a burden too heavy for her, her father's empty heart. Freed of that burden, her spirit spread its wings, and exacted devotion from a sea-horse.

It didn't matter to her who Kathleen was, or where she came from; if she had known that she was the sea-witch herself, she would have welcomed her with the same innocent joy. Half child, less than half woman, she was happy because she thought that I was happy.

Chris, too, rejoiced and in his own shy way made up to Kathleen with arch looks and fiery blushes and sudden leaps into the furniture. It was enough for both children that she was there;

it didn't occur to them that tomorrow she might not be. Chris was already planning tomorrow's adventures.

"Kathleen knows a place," he said, "where there's a big old lobster, and she said I could get him if I wanted." "Suppose he goes after you?" I asked; "what then?" "He wouldn't dass," said Chris, "because I'd shoot him dead." But he looked uneasy, and moved closer to Kathleen and took her hand. "Wouldn't I?" he asked.

He took heart again when Kathleen assured him that there was no danger. "Ah," he said, "he's only an old lobster."

"Maybe he has children," said Trisha, "and they'd be orphans."

I thought how little difference the death of an old lobster would make to his children, and how Trisha didn't know that; and then, suddenly, as I looked at mine, it struck me how a man's family sets him apart from all other living creatures. Who else has children he can call his own for longer than it takes to set them on their feet or on their way? The most loving animals, the vixen, the bear, the lioness, teach their cubs to make their own world, and to forget them; after the eagle has taught her eaglet to fly, she will see him no more. The spider bears her terrible children upon her back for a little while, but not for long; the wasp leaves her unborn daughter alone with a full larder, and that's as far as mother-love will take her. Calf, puppy, colt, grasshopper, dragon-fly, all go their separate ways as soon as they can; only man stands with his children from first to last, from birth to death, and to the grave.

Or—did Kathleen say—beyond it?

CHAPTER 10

THERE is no place in a child's book for a love story; everything is motion and adventure. That's why it's possible to write two or three children's books a year. There are only a few love stories in any man's life, and how many have a beginning and an end?

Kathleen and I walked on the beach together in the summer night. The half moon hung above us clear and lemon-silver in the sky and the waves broke like breaking crystal on the shore. There was a land wind, from the desert and the hills; it was warm, and smelled of sweet-grass. She wore a scarf of Trisha's around her hair, and she had an old jacket of mine over her shoulders. "It's beautiful, Lenny," she said. "I had no idea how beautiful everything is."

In the half-moonlight she seemed to drift along beside me like a wraith. I too felt shadowy; I couldn't see that either of us cast a shadow on the sand. "Kathleen," I said, half as a question, half in reassurance, and she put her hand in mine. It was firm and cool, and we walked that way together for a while.

"Did Chris really swim that far out with you?"

I asked after a time, and I could see her smile. "It wasn't really so far," she said; "he only thought it was." "It must have been far," I said; "he only swims a few strokes."

She stopped and looked at me steadily. "You don't believe in me, do you?" she said. "No," I said.

She turned as though to leave me, but I held her hand. "I don't know what to think," I said. She seemed sad, and a little weary. "Why do you have to think so much?" she asked. "Because I love you," I said.

She sighed, and stood staring at me for a long time. I had a feeling that she hadn't wanted this to happen, and that she dreaded what was to come. But a man knows when he is accepted, or rejected—though not always why. I opened my arms, and she came into them slowly, searching my face. Her mouth was sweet and fresh and seemed to melt into mine.

She pushed me away after a while like any mortal girl, and I saw that she was crying. I kissed her tears; they were salty, like all mortal tears. "Listen," I said; "I love you. Is that so bad?" She laughed a little shakily, and passed the back of her hand across her eyes. "Yes," she said; "it is."

I drew her down beside me on some dry sedge grass at the edge of the sand. I wanted to comfort her, to make it easy for her. "It doesn't have to be anything more than this," I said. "One summer night; but so lovely." "Yes," she said; "so lovely."

We sat in silence for a moment, looking up at the darkness and the stars, and she leaned her head against my shoulder. "This isn't real, Lenny," she said; "you know that, don't you?" "This moment is real," I said, "because we've made it so."

"You don't know who I am," she said.

I told her that it didn't matter, and at that moment I believed it. "I don't care who you are," I said, "or what you are." "Ah, Lenny," she said, "that's bold of you. But you don't know what it's like for me." "I only know how it is for me," I said, "when you're with me."

"You see," she said sadly, "it couldn't ever be one summer night. It wouldn't be enough. There's not time enough in it." "I know," I said, "I keep thinking that, too." "And what time have I?" she said. "I may not have very much." "I know that too," I said.

She put her arms around me and kissed me, and it was like the moonlight and the sweet-grass. I could feel her shiver in my arms. "Oh, Lenny," she breathed; "what are we going to do?"

I was cold, too, and I took a deep breath because I was afraid of what I had to ask her, and afraid of what she'd answer. "Will you marry me, Kathleen?" I asked, and waited, and held my breath, and heard my own heart beating in the stillness.

She turned away with a gesture of despair; she seemed to be struggling with some force outside of herself. The struggle, or the rebellion—or whatever it was—didn't last very long, and when she turned back and faced me again I knew that the answer was No.

I didn't ask her why; I think I'd known from the very first what the answer would be. There was only one thing I had to know. "Do you love me?" I asked; and she answered "Yes." Her voice was thin and far away; she sounded lost, and desolate.

I lay back and stared up at the night-blue bowl of the sky, silent and immense above me. I saw the darkness between the stars, those holes in time into which the little light of our own yesterdays flees forever without a sound, carrying our history with it. Yesterday, or a thousand years ago —it was all somewhere out there in the darkness, traveling at the speed of light toward ever distant suns. How little we know what lies beyond our sight, what eyes are watching.

I roused myself at last, and sat up, and took her hand; it was as cold as the sea. "At least," I said, "promise me not to vanish as you did before." "I promise," she said.

"Will you be always near me?" I asked; but she hesitated. "Always is such a big word," she said. "It's like forever. And who knows when forever is?"

"Forever is tomorrow," I said; "tomorrow and tomorrow." "It's yesterday, too," said Kathleen gently.

I knew that she was thinking of Trina, and it was like a cloud across the night. "Forget yesterday," I said, and my voice sounded rough and hoarse in my own ears; "there's room for more than one love in a man's life."

I thought that she looked at me strangely, and sadly too. "Is there?" she asked. "Then you haven't understood."

She stood up, and drew my jacket closer around her shoulders. "All right," she said; "forget yesterday."

I glanced up at her in surprise. She was so young, standing there, erect and slender in the night, so young and so vulnerable. There was something hurt and bitter in the way she stood there. "What about Alice?" she asked.

The question took me by surprise. "Alice who?" I asked stupidly, and she gave a light laugh, like a jealous child. "I don't know," she said; "you didn't tell me."

"Are you serious?" I asked. "I scarcely know her." She laughed again, but there was a little break in it. "Tomorrow and tomorrow," she said. "There's room for more than one love in a man's life. You said so yourself."

It was so absurd that I had to laugh. Her whole mood had changed; This was no creature without a shadow, out of a mystery or the sea; this was a mortal girl ruffling her feathers against an imagined rival. "Kathleen!" I cried, turning to grasp her, but my hands closed on empty air. Already she was running down the beach, flitting along like a sandpiper, and not looking back. My jacket trailed from her shoulders; and presently it fell off onto the sand.

When I caught up with her, she was sitting on a rock by the water's edge, looking dejectedly out to sea. "I suppose if I hadn't caught you," I said, trying to get my breath, "you'd have vanished again." She looked up at me and shook her head. "No," she said; "not any more."

I folded my jacket around her shoulders, and she drew it tight, not so much for warmth as though she wanted to hide in it. "Are you angry?" she asked in a small voice. "I am so ashamed of myself."

I told her that I wasn't angry; that on the contrary, her behavior—which reminded me of Trisha in one of her moods—enchanted me. She made a little sound of distress. "Now you are laughing at me," she said, "and that's even worse, I think."

"No, truly, I am not," I said.

"I don't know what came over me," she said. "I was afraid. . . . There was tomorrow, waiting for you—and I wasn't part of it."

"Lovers are like that," I told her, but she refused to believe it. "Would any other girl be jealous so soon?" she asked. And she added decidedly: "Besides—we're not lovers."

"What else are we, then?" I asked. "Yes," she said in a low voice; "what else?

"Ah me." She bent her head and rubbed her cheek against my hand. "I'm trying so hard to understand," I said. "I, too," she whispered.

She drew a deep sigh, and laid her head against my breast. "I'm very unhappy," she said.

I stroked her hair that was cold as night,

"Look," I began uncertainly: "if all this makes you so unhappy . . ." I stopped, because I realized suddenly that I couldn't say it. I couldn't say: "we'll not see each other any more." I couldn't even bear to think of it.

I didn't have to. "It isn't that," she said; "it's only that I'm not used to being happy. And now I'm happy and unhappy too."

And she added mournfully:

"I've never been in love before."

There is something about sadness in love that is more real than joy, even. Whatever fears and doubts I'd had, melted away; I felt suddenly light and tall and ready to undertake anything, to promise anything. It was no ghost sitting there at my side, but a young girl in her first sorrowful surrender; and if she was enchanted, then the night and I were enchanted, too. I thought—in that tall moment—that it wouldn't make any difference, anyway. All love is an enchantment, and makes a hero of a frog, or an Empress of a courtesan. Without it, I was only a writer of children's stories.

She got up slowly, and turned, holding out her hands to me in a gesture pleading and childlike. "Can't we take each other for what we are?" she said, "without asking what we'll be tomorrow?"

"Tell me that you'll love me," I demanded, "at least till then." "It may not be for very long," she said. "My shadow is light on the earth."

"Then for what it's worth," I said, "tell me." "For what it's worth," she said, "I'll love you tomorrow and tomorrow and tomorrow."

We went slowly back to the house together, up the hill from the sea; and the low moon made a path in the water between my house and China.

We were together all night. She was new to love, and it was a glory and a wonder to her. We fell asleep in each other's arms, and woke again, and slept, and woke, and watched the dawn come up over the hills and spread itself across the sea. We breathed the cold, fresh morning air; it was a new day, a golden day. We laughed at nothing and at each other; we cooked fried eggs on the stove in the chilled, dawn-gray kitchen, and ate them with bread and honey.

Morning lay like a pearl on the sea when we went down to swim. It was full day when we came back to the house, and the children were awake.

CHAPTER 11

THERE began then, for me, a period of enchantment. I don't know what else to call it; perhaps I can best describe it by saying that I woke each day into a new, bright, morning world, and that it was the same world I had known once before.

I was happy, I was no longer lonely. And sometimes I had a curious feeling that Trina was happy too; happy for me, and happy for herself. Perhaps, if she had lived, we might have had as much pure joy together, but even so, it wouldn't have been the same. You make your peace with marriage; the lover becomes a husband and a father; morning becomes noon, a deeper light.

The children accepted Kathleen as a natural part of their lives. Neither Chris nor Trisha ever spoke of her again in connection with their mother; they were only anxious that she shouldn't ever leave us. "Can't she stay with us always?" Trisha asked. I could not reply.

Kathleen said nothing, now, about leaving me. She found a little house on the beach near our own, and after signing a year's lease, moved in. It had been empty for quite a long while, and dust lay all over; it had a roof which had obviously leaked during the winter rains, but Kathleen was delighted with it. I found her sweeping the floor with an old broom, and Trisha's scarf over her hair. "See," she said happily, "it has a fireplace and a stove, and there's a room for my bed, and a dresser; and it is only a little walk from here to your house." "Do you have a bed?" I asked, "and a dresser?" Her face fell. "No," she said. "I thought maybe you would have an extra one."

We found a bed and a dresser, by letting the two children sleep together in my room, and my taking Trisha's room and giving Kathleen Chris's bed and Trisha's dresser. We carried them down to her house the next day, along with a few kitchen utensils and a blanket. She told us she had her own linen and silver.

Already the little house was transformed. She had laid mats of woven rushes on the floor, and she had brought in branches of coral, rosy shells, and screens of driftwood inlaid with mother of pearl. She had made a table of a sea-washed plank, and she had hung curtains at the windows of dyed tapa cloth. Her linen, which she showed us proudly, was very old and fine, and so was her silver, some of which showed the royal arms of Spain, and some the Lion and Unicorn of England. The little house glowed with her treasures, and she glowed too, looking around her with such a childish joy that one would have thought she had never had a house of her own before.

Uncle Harry Cole came down to look it over from his own shack in Nichols Canyon in the hills above us. I could see that he was surprised. "Well, now," he said, drawing me aside; "this looks like a real home." "What do you think," I said, smiling; "shall I throw her back into the sea?"

He didn't answer right away as I expected; instead, he looked grave, and pursed his lips. "I do believe," he said at last, "I'd think twice about that." "Aren't you afraid for me any more?" I asked. "By God," he said, "I don't know. I think I'm more afraid for her, now I've had a good look at her."

We left the children to help Kathleen in the house, and walked out along the beach. "It's a funny thing," he said; "I didn't know was she real or not before, and I still don't know. But maybe it doesn't matter. There's a world of things around us we don't see for what they are. I loved a woman once that held me to be a grunion."

"I know," I said. "You told me." "What I mean is," he said, "she was no more woman than that tussock over there. But I kept seeing her as a woman for quite a while. It was the way I thought of her. Well, by God, I was as far off the truth as from here to the equator."

"I don't know what the truth is, Uncle Harry," I said.

"Somebody loves you in the world," said Uncle Harry, "or out of it, and that's the truth."

What I had now from Kathleen was not only love and companionship, it was the union of a gentle spirit to mine. Except for the hours at my desk—for I still had a book to write—we were with each other most of the time. After breakfast, the children went pelting down the hill to her house to spend the morning with her, while I worked: Trisha no longer cut out her paper dolls beside me as I wrote. At noon all three came up to lunch, and we spent the afternoons on the beach together, lying in the sun and swimming in the sea.

I was alarmed at first to see the children go so far out with her beyond the breakers, but after a while I grew used to it and didn't worry any more. We were together in the blue dusk of evening; sometimes she cooked our dinner for us, sometimes I did; sometimes, when the children had gone to sleep, we listened to music from the record player and sat before the fire and dreamed. Or we walked along the beach under the night sky, watching the white surf rising and falling in the darkness, listening to the waves foaming at our feet; the sandpipers who should have been asleep went with us, flitting ahead of us like little shadows.

Once we heard an owl hooting in the hills behind us, and I felt Kathleen shiver and press closer to me. "It's such a lonely sound," she said.

A little later she said: "Do you know what it is

to be all alone in the world? With no one to belong to?"

Still later she said: "How do you belong to someone? I want so terribly to belong to you." "You do," I said, but she only shook her head. "That isn't what I mean," she said.

At another time she asked me to tell her about Trina. "Did you love her very much?" she asked. I told her yes, very much, and she seemed pleased. "Am I like her?" she asked; and when I told her she was very much like her, it made her happy. "I feel as though I were," she said. "I think she wants me to be.

"She loved you very much," she said gently. "And so do I."

But often we said nothing, content merely to be together, or we said the small things that people say when they're happy. I took Kathleen marketing at Trancas; we joined Uncle Harry Cole surf-fishing along the shore (she named a strange-looking fish which Uncle Harry caught, and which no one recognized; it was, she told him, a kelp fish); and each time he caught a perch, she asked to be allowed to throw it back into the sea again, and whispered something to it before she let it go. When I asked her what she was whispering, she first blushed and looked guilty, and then she laughed. "I'm telling it that these are the rewards of greediness," she said.

But she never wanted to go beyond Trancas, or to the city itself; and so, when Mr. Goldberg called for me to come in again, I went alone.

I met Dick at the Sportsmen's Lodge, and he had Alice with him. Only this time it was different. "You look wonderful, Lenny," he said. "Did you find your girl?" "Yes," I said, "I found her.

And her name is Kathleen, and she's not a seal."
He laughed, and slapped me fondly on the shoulder. "I'm glad," he said. Then he said, simply:
"Alice and I are going to be married."

I gaped at them in surprise; it was a shock to me at first; I'd never have thought that Alice was Dick's kind of woman, she struck me as being too light-headed. But after all, what did I know about her? Whatever there was in the girl, good or bad, could only be known to the man she belonged to. I could hear Uncle Harry again: "There's a world of things around us we don't see for what they are." "Well!" I said; "congratulations!"

We had a drink on it, all three of us clinking our glasses, and I told them they'd have to come down to the beach to meet Kathleen. "We'll have that picnic we were talking about," I said. Dick's eyebrows went up. "You sure she'll be there?"

he asked. "She'll be there," I said, "unless she's turned into a sandpiper."

But I felt sad. It was going to be so easy for Dick and Alice.

"Did you find out when her birthday was?" asked Alice. I looked at her blankly. "Do you know," I said; "I forgot all about it." "It's very important," she said seriously, "when you're going to get married, to know when your birthday is."

Toward the end of lunch I asked Dick if he knew what Mr. Goldberg wanted to see me about, and his manner changed; he looked mournful and uneasy. "I don't think he likes the story any more, Lenny," he said. "I think he wants to give it up." "Can he do that?" I asked innocently. "Sure," said Dick; "why not? All he has is an option."

When we got to Mr. Goldberg's office, the little producer looked mournful, too. "Lenny, Baby," he said, "you got to understand this. Personally, I like your story very much; but I'm going to have to give it back to you." "Why?" I asked. "What's the matter with it?" "The matter with it," said Mr. Goldberg morosely, "is it's a love story. You know, and I know, we got to have love; but how many other people know? How many people got romance in their lives? I was afraid of that, right away; remember? It's understandable; I, for one, understand it."

He rose heavily from his desk, and patted me on the arm. "I'm sorry, Baby," he said; "I just can't sell the idea upstairs. They say it's too gentle. Love with passion—yes: with suspense, with faces in the window. From somewhere should come a shot, or some nervous trouble; otherwise the Trendex rating is 5.1, like Shakespeare."

We went back to the Lodge, and had a drink. I should have been feeling bad, but I wasn't; it didn't seem to matter any more. "That's how it is in television," said Dick. "There's always someone further upstairs." "Just the same," I said, "without love, what have you got? What does a man have more than a cricket? Only love. They both got troubles."

I was talking like Mr. Goldberg, and enjoying it. "What does astrology say about me lately?" I asked Alice. She fished in her handbag, and brought out a folded piece of newspaper, with the day's horoscope on it. "Let me see," she said. "Virgo . . . no, that's me . . . 'favorable contacts' . . . Here it is: Capricorn. 'Those in authority are watching you. . . .' That's what it says, honey." "I know," I said. "I know they are."

"One more drink?" asked Dick; "a last one for the road?" "One for the road," I said, "and one for Baby."

"Don't forget to ask her when her birthday is," said Alice. "I won't forget," I said, "but I don't think she'll tell me."

It was good to come home and find the house without that empty look any more, but warm and humming the way it used to be. Kathleen was in the kitchen; Trisha was setting the table, and Chris was hunting imaginary dragons with his space gun. The children came pelting out to the car, wanting to know if the next check had come, and if I had brought it home with me. When I told them no, their faces fell, but only for a moment. They were happy enough with what they had, and made few demands: if they were disappointed today, there was always tomorrow.

I said to Kathleen that night: "I'm sorry for Mr. Goldberg. He's a nice little man, and he's caught in a formula. The people upstairs have the answer, and it isn't love."

"You don't believe that, do you?" she asked. "No," I said. "And neither does Alice." "Oh," she said in a small voice; "was she there, too?" "I had lunch with her," I said.

She started to get up, but I held on to her. "Dick was there," I said. "He and Alice are going to be married."

Her face lit up. "Oh, how wonderful," she cried. "How beautiful for them." A moment later she was weeping.

I left her to cry; there wasn't anything else I could do. There was no way to comfort her. Or myself.

Later she came to me in an apologetic mood.

"I'm sorry," she said. "It's like a woman to want the best of both worlds." "Yes," I said, "it's like a woman." I could see her thinking about it, turning it over in her mind. "Thank you for that," she said gently.

She stood on tiptoe and kissed me on the mouth. "That's the answer," she said; "not what they think upstairs."

It was the only answer for me, anyway. I was sorry about the money, because I could have bought her something, and I told her so. "That's dear of you," she said, "but what would I have done with it? I have everything."

She had nothing, really; and I had little enough, but I felt the same way about it. We had enough for our needs, and for the children—or I had; and we had each other, at least until tomorrow. We weren't planning on a bright future, or a long life together. The few little gifts I'd given her didn't amount to much, and what she gave me were things of her own: a Spanish coin, a piece of amber, a gold signet ring. Her clothes struck me as strange at times, and old-fashioned at others, but where they came from I never asked. All I knew was, she was beautiful in anything, and it made me happy to tell her so. It made her happy, too, though she always turned shy when I told her, as if she didn't believe me. Perhaps she didn't. Trina had been like that, but Trina was never what you'd call beautiful.

Or was she? Strange: I must have thought her so at one time; but I grew used to it. On the other hand, I hadn't thought Kathleen beautiful at first; that came later, and seemed to grow out of being in love with her. Why hadn't it happened that way with Trina, whom I had loved too? Life itself must have worn that beauty away. Whereas with Kathleen each day was like a little season of its own, and only the beach and the sea made up our world—as far removed from the life around us as though we were on another planet. There was no way that summer to grow used to beauty.

We planned our picnic for Dick and Alice, but first I had to get a permit from the authorities to make a fire on the beach. It wasn't easy to get, the season being so dry and the danger of brush fires in the hills so great. But I promised to keep my fire below the high tide mark, and after grumbling a bit they gave it to me.

I don't know who was more excited, the children or Kathleen. She was like a child herself, giving her first party, and everything had to be perfect. She wanted to know what to cook, what to buy, what to bring in from the sea, what to wear

. . . it was obviously, in her mind, an important occasion.

I tried to get her to see that it was only a picnic for some friends. "All we need, really," I said, "are frankfurters and beer. And marshmallows for the children, to toast in the fire."

She gave me a stricken look. "You're making it seem just ordinary," she said, "and I wanted it to be wonderful."

We set a date with Dick and Alice for the following week when the tide would be right, and Chris and Kathleen went fishing for lobsters. Trisha stayed at home and baked a cake; it was a little soggy, and leaned a bit to one side, and she was doubtful about it. "Never mind," I said; "maybe it will straighten itself out before the party." But she had another solution which she thought more appealing. "Maybe if I eat some of it now," she said, "people won't see how leany it is."

I had to tell her that she couldn't wear her new dress to the picnic. It was a great blow to her, and for a whole day she went around looking sorry for herself. "I'll never get to wear it," she said plaintively. "I'll be a grown-up woman before I get to wear it. What good is it?"

She cheered up a little when I assured her that nobody ever wore her best clothes to the beach. "Well, all right," she said; "but there's no use having any, if nobody ever sees them." "Next winter," I said, "I'll take you to dinner in town, and you can dress up like a Christmas tree." "We'll have to wait till the next check comes in," she said, "and I'll be an old woman."

I drove up into Nichols Canyon to invite Old Uncle Harry Cole to the party, and I noticed how dry it was up there in the hills. It was a bad place, that canyon; a fire could spread there in a hurry. I wouldn't want to be caught in it.

On the way back, I stopped at Trancas and bought a green scarf for Kathleen's hair, and some frankfurters.

CHAPTER 12

IT was a fine picnic. Alice came dressed in slacks, which greatly relieved Trisha's mind, and Dick brought Mr. Goldberg with him, which I didn't expect. Uncle Harry Cole came down from his canyon with a bottle of bourbon, and we had lobsters and corn and Trisha's cake, or what was left of it, and frankfurters and beer and marshmallows and milk, and potatoes burned black on the outside, hot, and crackling, and apple-sweet. The tide was out; beyond the yellow firelight the surf rose up out of the darkness in ghostly foam, and fell in a dim, white smother among the rocks. The moon lay over us, small and round and silver and far away.

The children were drawn by the fire, and sat as close to it as they could get, gazing into the flames with dreamy eyes. "I love a fire," said Trisha; "it makes me sleepy." "This is a very good fire," said Chris; "I bet they can see it in China." "They can't see it in China, silly," said Trisha; "it's on the upside-down side of the earth."

"Well," said Chris stubbornly, "they can see it on the moon." "They can't either," said Trisha decidedly. "Why not?" asked Chris. "We can see them; why can't they see us?" "Because there's nothing on the moon," said Trisha, wrinkling up her nose in disgust, "except spidery horrors."

Alice, lying with her head against Dick's shoulder, shivered delicately. "I don't like spiders," she said; "I have a thing about them. I don't mind big things, but little things scare me." "I don't scare you," said Trisha, "and I'm only little."

"The biggest things are usually gentle," said Kathleen, "unless they're hungry, or frightened. You take the whale, he doesn't want to hurt anybody. Even the giant squid won't hurt you, unless he's frightened. Or hungry," she added.

"What's a giant squid got to be afraid of?" asked Uncle Harry Cole; "a thing like that?" "I knew one once," said Kathleen. "He wasn't afraid of anything. But he was hungry all the time."

There was a little silence, and I saw Dick and Alice look at each other, and then turn and look at Kathleen. Uncle Harry Cole saw it too, and cleared his throat. "Well, now," he said gently, "I expect he had a large stomach to feed." "He was all stomach," said Kathleen simply. "Except his arms, of course.

"People are the only ones who hurt each other for the fun of it."

Alice declared that she didn't think it was much fun to hurt people. "I try to live by the golden rule," she said, "and by what my chart tells me every day. Astrology," she said in answer to Kathleen's inquiring look: "my Horoscope."

And leaning forward on one elbow, she explained to Kathleen that she followed the advice of the stars. "That's how we're going to be married," she said: "when the stars are favorable. Tell me when your birthday is, and I'll tell you what Sign you're under; or do you know?"

Kathleen shook her head. "I don't know what Sign I'm under," she said. "I don't know when I was born, it was so long ago." "It couldn't have been so long ago," said Alice. She studied Kathleen for a moment, her head cocked to one side. "I've got an idea you're an Aquarius," she said finally. "Am I right?" "I don't know," said Kathleen.

I was glad that she and Alice seemed to be getting along together. I wanted everyone to like her. Trina had been liked so much; I wanted it for Kathleen.

The fire made a warm, rosy place for us in the night. The hills rose up behind us, and the night stood around us, silvered by the moon. I thought of our fire being seen all the way to China; China had been one of the strange, far-off, exciting places in the world, and now you couldn't think of it any more. There weren't very many places left. "I used to dream I'd go to China one day," I said; "right out over the edge of the world." "You like to dream, don't you, Baby?" said Mr. Goldberg.

Maybe I did, but I didn't want to talk about it, not there. "It's a living," I said lightly, and shrugged my shoulders. But Mr. Goldberg had serious things on his mind. "I suppose we got to dream, in our business," he said; "but the way I see it, dreams don't tell people how to get along in life."

I looked helplessly around, wanting somebody to say something to keep the discussion from getting too serious. I thought maybe Alice would say that the stars could tell them how, and I looked over at her, but she was gazing up at Dick. "It isn't life they've got to get along with," said Dick, "it's death. That's what scares them."

So there goes the evening, I thought. I didn't want to talk about death, with the fire there in front of us and the moon over us. Besides, death didn't ride with them the way it did with me.

But Mr. Goldberg wanted to talk about it; the blood of his ancestors, great questioners and argufiers, ran in his veins. "Do you believe in the hereafter, Lenny?" he asked.

I shook my head. "I don't have the answer to that one," I admitted.

It didn't satisfy him, as I knew it wouldn't. "Come," he said, "you can do better than that." "All right, then," I said: "the way I look at it is this: I don't know what's out there beyond the stars. But I know that whatever it is, we've got to get along with it. And I know something else: we've got one thing working for us, and that is love."

"That's nice poetry, Lenny," said Mr. Goldberg, "and I understand it. But would sixty million people understand it?" "Yes," I said; "I think they would." "They don't think so upstairs," said Mr. Goldberg.

Alice let her head sink back on Dick's shoulder. "I like to think that love comes from beyond," she said drowsily.

"Beyond what?" asked Mr. Goldberg. "I don't know," she said. "Just beyond."

"All right," said Mr. Goldberg mildly: "love comes from beyond. You say so, and I buy it. But love is easy to get along with. Our friend Dick here says that what we have to get along with is death, and this is not easy; and this, also, I buy.

Only, now I ask him: from where comes death?"

He peered around the circle of firelight, but no one answered. The fire shook a sudden shower of sparks into the air. "I carry it in my bones," he said, "and you would think my bones and I would get along together. Maybe love should not be so far away; so death would not be so lonely."

I glanced across at Kathleen, and she was looking at me, with the firelight rosy on her face. "Love has been known to follow death," she said. "Is that an answer?" asked Mr. Goldberg. "Yes," she said.

Warmed by the bourbon and the fire, Uncle Harry Cole leaned forward and held his bottle up to the light. "Beyond is beyond," he said. "There's valleys in the sea, and spaces between the stars no mortal man has ever laid eyes on. He can see them in his mind. But there's a beyond that the mind can't see; and that's where the answers are."

We were silent for a moment, listening to the little crackle of the fire, and the sound of the waves breaking on the shore. Well, I thought, we're serious, all right. I looked at the children; they were already half asleep. "Yes, sir," said Uncle Harry, "we'll probably know all about those starry spaces some day, we'll travel in them. And we'll go down into the valleys of the sea, and look around. But what lies out there beyond the mind—that we'll never know."

Mr. Goldberg traced a figure in the sand at his feet. "Men have one death," he said, "but sometimes many loves. How can that be, if death still has its love?" "Don't ask me," said Uncle Harry, lifting the bottle to his lips. "I never had but one, and I was wrong about her."

The little producer turned to Kathleen. "What

do you think, Miss Kathleen?" he asked. "Is it possible to love more than once?"

She looked across at me, and smiled, and her eyes caught the firelight and shone green. "The body renews itself," she said gently: "why not the heart?"

I could see that he was puzzled. "Am I renewed?" he asked plaintively. "I am still the same Goldberg which I see every day if I look. So what is the change? It is still the same body." "It is still the same heart," said Kathleen. "That doesn't change, either."

The same heart, I thought; and the same love. The heart that loves Kathleen, and that Trina loves.

I looked at Uncle Harry Cole; he was staring at Kathleen across the fire, and his face was humble and thoughtful. "So that's it," he said: "if a man takes it with him when he goes . . .

"Well, by God," he said, "I expect he can send it back again."

Kathleen's head was bent, she seemed to be studying the sand under her fingers, lifting a little at a time and letting it sift idly down again. "Do you mean," Alice asked, "that if a man loved a woman enough, he might come back to her? Like a ghost?" "No," said Kathleen; "not like a ghost."

She didn't look at me, but I knew that she was speaking to me, and only me. I think that Uncle Harry Cole knew it too. "There's the word, Lenny," he said.

Alice settled back with a thankful sigh. "You had me scared for a minute," she said. "I thought you meant a ghost."

And she added, with a little laugh:

"When Lenny first told us about you, we thought you were a seal."

Kathleen laughed too, a sweet, easy laugh, and we all laughed, and that was that, and afterwards it was like any other night for lovers, with the fire-smell and the sea-smell, and the pale moon sailing over us.

Uncle Harry Cole told us stories about the sea, and Mr. Goldberg told us about his early days as a song writer. Dick and Alice didn't talk much; they drank beer together out of a can, and gazed up at the stars. "There's Jupiter," said Alice; "that's Dick's planet; and mine is Mercury." "Jupiter," said Dick: "the power and the glory." "I like the evening star best," I said.

" 'Bright Star, would I were stedfast as thou art—
'Not in lone splendour hung aloft the night . . .' "

. . .

We sat around the fire and sang in the soft summer night, the old songs, "Juanita," "Sweet and Low," "Believe Me If All Those Endearing Young Charms" . . .

> 'No, the heart that has truly lov'd never forgets,
> 'But as truly loves on to the close . . .'

while the embers died and the moon rode through the sky, and the children slept under their blanket. A plane drummed through the night, far out above the black water, its red lights winking on and off. A sandpiper skittered along the beach, at the sea's edge. Alice lay smiling with her head on Dick's shoulder, and I held Kathleen, warm and dear and for a while mortal, in my arms.

CHAPTER 13

It was three or four days later that Kathleen told me she wanted to give Dick and Alice their wedding at our house. She was telling the children a story when I came in, and I stood in the doorway watching. She sat at the foot of Trisha's bed, her hair in a witch-cloud around her shoulders, and the two little faces looked up at her with round eyes from under the bedclothes.

It was the story of a little dog who was sent up into the sky in a balloon, and sailed around and around the earth, looking down at it. "He saw the oceans," she said, "all blue beneath him, and the great continents lying in the water like stones in a pond, green and brown, and white with snow. And he saw the countries and the rivers and the cities, and he saw his own country, and his own city, and his own house where he lived with his master, Dr. Kubie, and Helen the housekeeper, and Lee Sharon, the housekeeper's daughter, and Tabitha the cat. He remembered how he used to have a rubber ball to play with, and he remembered the clean bones, and the clear water, and man's love, and afternoon tea. He was very lonely up there in the sky all by himself, and he was afraid he'd never get home again. And he thought, if only there was some way to send my regards to my family and my friends. Just then a sparrow came flying past, and stopped and asked him why he was so sad, and what he was doing up there in the sky in a balloon, and where he was going. 'Alas,' said the little dog, 'nobody told me where I was going, or what I was supposed to do; and I am sad because I am all alone here, far from those I love, and I wish I could send them my regards.' 'I'd be glad to take your regards to them,' said the sparrow, 'if it is not too far out of my way.' So the little dog very eagerly sent his regards and his love to Dr. Kubie and Lee Sharon and Helen the housekeeper and Tabitha the cat, and to clean bones and clear water and rubber balls and afternoon tea, at number 12, Andover Road, Beverly, Massachusetts. 'I wasn't planning to go to Massachusetts,' said the sparrow, 'because my connections are all in New Jersey'; but when he saw how the little dog's face fell and how disappointed he was, he said, 'I will go to Beverly anyway, and give them your message.' So the sparrow flew down to earth, and the little dog went sailing on around the sky, but he was happier now because his family and his friends would know that he loved them."

Trisha's eyes, which had been like saucers at first, were almost closed. "What happened to the sparrow?" she asked sleepily. "The sparrow?" said Kathleen lightly; "why, they all said thank you very much and asked him in to tea." "I baked him a cake," murmured Trisha, and mumbled her prayers: "Now I lay me down to sleep, I pray the Lord my soul to keep . . ." She had a long list of blessings, including Old Uncle Harry Cole and Mr. Goldberg, "and God bless Dr. Kubie and Lee Sharon and Helen and Tabitha the cat and the little dog and the sparrow . . ."

"Thank you," said Kathleen, and dropped a

kiss on Trisha's cheek as she fell asleep. Chris, with a much shorter list, was sleeping already.

Kathleen came out and closed the door behind her. "Lenny," she said, "I wish we could give the Bassets their wedding. Here, in this house, I mean, or in mine. Do you think they'd like it? Or do they have a lot of friends . . . ?" "I think they'd love it," I said. "Anyway, I can ask." "Of course," she said, hesitating, "if they were planning a church wedding . . ." "If I know Dick," I said, "they were probably going before a justice of the peace.

"They'd want to ask a few people," I said, "but we could manage that. The only thing is . . ." I stopped, because I didn't know just how to say it. "I mean," I said, "are you sure you want to?"

She looked at me, almost in surprise, I thought. "Yes," she said; "of course I'm sure. Why not?"

I didn't want to tell her why not; I didn't want to tell her that I thought it would make her sad. To have to watch, like that, what she could never share. . . . But I didn't know my Kathleen. She had no envy in her heart.

There was still one other difficulty: my next check hadn't come, and I had no money for the expenses. Kathleen went down to her house, and after a while she came back with a necklace, and put it in my hand. "Sell it," she said. "It will pay for the refreshments."

It was a beautiful necklace, and it looked old and valuable. "This is a very rare piece," the jeweler said when I took it in to him the next day: "it really belongs in a museum. It's what we call gem coral, and it's quite flawless, and a fine color. I'm afraid I can't buy it myself, but if you'd care to leave it with me, I might be able to find a purchaser for it." He held the necklace up to the light and turned it this way and that, admiring it. "There is a description of a necklace like this," he said, "in the *Memoires* of Ninon de L'Enclos. It belonged to a friend of hers, a Mrs. Wibberley, an Irish lady who was drowned at sea in 1687. It's the first time I've ever seen another like it."

I told him to keep it until he found a purchaser, and to give me a small down-payment, enough for the champagne and the flowers. He gave me a hundred dollars, and I telephoned Dick. "Kathleen wants you to have your wedding at our house," I said. "I'll have to ask Alice," he declared; "we were going to Las Vegas." "How do you feel about it yourself?" I asked. "I'd love it at your house," he said.

Alice thought she'd love it, too. "I like your girl," she said; "I think she's sweet. Maybe some day we'll do the same for you." "Sure," I said; "sure. Maybe some day."

Dick gave me a list of guests and the name of the minister at the Church of The Living God which Alice had attended a few times, and we sent out the invitations and ordered the champagne and the flowers and the chicken salad and the wedding cake.

I had never seen Kathleen as happy as she was those few days before the ceremony. She was so happy she made me feel happy too. She was like a dancer on tiptoe waiting in the wings, breathless with anticipation. "It's going to be so lovely, Lenny," she said; "it's going to be so beautiful."

The day of the wedding was sunny, and the afternoon warm. Because the ceremony was being held in my house, and because I wanted to be with Kathleen during it, I had asked Uncle Harry Cole to hold the ring for Dick, and Alice had asked Mr. Goldberg to give the bride away. Trisha was to be flower girl; the new dress had been brought out and put on at last, and she wore a little wreath of rosebuds in her hair. How proud and shy she was! Chris had been invited to help with the refreshments, and had already stuck his finger into the icing on the wedding cake.

Only the minister was strange. The pastor of Alice's church had been taken ill, and another had come in his place. He was a heavy-set, rough-bearded man, uncomfortable in his clothes, with deep-set eyes; I thought of Proteus rising from the sea, or Triton and his horn. None of the guests appeared to know him, and I noticed that Kathleen steered away from him whenever she could. She looked troubled, but when I asked her if anything was wrong, she shook her head. I thought perhaps she was worried about the wedding not going off all right. "Throw some salt over your left shoulder," I told her, "and keep your fingers crossed." She gave me a tight little smile, and touched my cheek with her hand, the way she always did. "I'll do that," she said; but she looked concerned.

It was a lovely wedding. The house was filled with flowers, and the sea lay blue as the sky outside our windows. I stood with Kathleen among the guests, and our bodies touched, and we held hands together. "Darling," she whispered; "darling." It was the only time she had ever called me that. "It is beautiful," she whispered. "It's the way I thought it would be."

The minister had asked the usual questions; and then, surprisingly, he turned his back on the room, and looked out over the sea. I heard Kathleen give a little gasp, and stiffen suddenly at my side, as though she saw something that no one else saw. "Already?" she breathed. "Is it so late?"

I glanced at her, and I thought she looked pale. "What is it?" I asked. The minister had turned back again, and I had a feeling that he was looking at us. "Hush," she whispered; "hush."

He was speaking now in his deep voice that had the sound of distant shores and the wind; and he was looking at us, and speaking to us.

"Dearly Beloved," he said, "you have joined hands upon a road where each one goes, together or apart. It is the road of life, and you have chosen to take it together. It is not an easy road, for it crosses sandy wastes and stony fields; but your feet were set upon it by those who went before you, and you have no choice but to follow it to the end.

"Nevertheless, follow it with courage and joy, for you have many friends. About you and around you the air, the earth, and the sea are filled with God's creatures. They are not always visible; many are exquisite and ethereal beings."

I felt Kathleen's hand tremble in mine. "I know him now," she whispered. "Oh, Lenny . . . !"

"These bright invisible beings," the minister went on "are God's messengers. Their names are love. They come and go, between today and yesterday. They are sent to tell you that even among the galaxies of heaven, man is not forgotten.

"But they are not yours to keep; they cannot stay. They are sent out, and they are called home again. Treasure them; and when the time comes, return them whence they came, to the air, to the earth, and to the sea. For all things return to the elements of which they are composed; and must be so returned.

"So love returns, to love.

"From the marriage of insects, other insects are born; the swift, shy birds give birth to winged forms from whom the same sweet songs ascend. From the wedding of minds, new thoughts are conceived. And from the wedding of souls, love goes forth into the universe.

"All marriages are fruitful. May this, too, be fruitful: of understanding, and peace."

The adjuration came to an end, and Kathleen was quiet at my side; she scarcely seemed to breathe. I felt her hand withdraw itself gently from my clasp, and when I turned to look at her, I saw that her cheeks were wet.

"I now by the authority invested in me . . ." The ceremony was over. Mr. Goldberg was shaking Dick by the hand, and Uncle Harry Cole was kissing the bride. The other guests crowded forward, and Kathleen and I were left alone.

I took her in my arms, although I didn't know it, for the last time. "Lenny," she whispered; "my love." I kissed her wet eyes and her mouth for the last time. "Hold me a moment," she said, "and then I must go." I said that I'd go with her, but she shook her head. "No," she said; "I have things to do."

She seemed composed, gentle and gay again, as though she had gotten over whatever it was that had grieved her. "You have work to do, too," she said. "You have things to do here."

Chris came up to me at that moment and tugged at my knee. "Can I serve the refreshments now?" he asked. "Can I?" I turned to tell him yes, and when I turned back to Kathleen, she was gone.

I thought she might have stepped into the kitchen, to make sure of the arrangements, and as soon as I had congratulated the bride and groom, I went to look for her. But she wasn't there. She wasn't in the kitchen. She wasn't anywhere.

I went back to my duties as host, but my mind wasn't on it. I kept wondering where she was. Had she slipped away to her own little house—to cry a little, perhaps—like any woman? I had expected that. But why didn't she come back?

The afternoon went on and on, interminably. Dick and Alice left in a shower of laughter and rice; the minister had disappeared long since, apparently without saying good-bye to anyone. Trisha and Chris kept running in and out of the kitchen with plates of food, and I kept filling the glasses, but we needed Kathleen, we missed her. "I don't know where the spoons are," said Chris. "I don't know where anything is." And Trisha kept looking for Kathleen to pin the wreath of roses more securely in her hair.

The daylight began to fade, the lamps were lit. Uncle Harry Cole and Mr. Goldberg were the last to leave, and I saw them to the door. "Say goodbye to your sweet girl for me," said Mr. Goldberg. "I haven't seen her around."

Uncle Harry Cole shook hands with me. "It was a good wedding," he said. "A little strange, maybe. I kept waiting for the Twenty-third Psalm."

I watched them go up the hill to the road. There was a gray fog rolling in from the sea. It hid the beach; I couldn't see Kathleen's little house at all.

I went down the hill, and when I got to the fog it was wet and icy, as though it had come up from the depths of ocean. I called Kathleen's name, but there was no answer.

The house, when I got to it, was empty. All the curtains were gone from the windows, the woven mats from the floor. The screens inlaid with mother-of-pearl, the corals, the shells, all were gone; only the bed and the dresser stood there in the bare room, with the dust-smell, and the fog, and the sound of the sea outside.

It was then I heard the crying. At first I thought it was my own, but it came from somewhere in the fog, far out, in the direction of the sea. It was a sound of weeping, the loneliest sound I ever heard.

I walked down to the water. Everywhere in the sand were the marks of sandpipers.

CHAPTER 14

THERE isn't much more to tell. I had no feeling at all at first, beyond the sense of emptiness and loss; but that's the way it is with a wound, if it's deep enough, it hurts afterwards. The first thing is the shock, and the unbelief; and then, when it begins to heal, you feel the pain. I felt forsaken, and this time without hope; for a while I tried to forget, to put my mind on other things, but there were no other things. Later, I tried to remember, to comfort myself with memories. I tried to understand, I wanted so much to understand. I wanted Kathleen to come back to me.

She never did come back. But there was a time when the sense of her presence returned to me, and I felt less forsaken. It was after a night late in summer, when coming into Trisha's room where she was sleeping, I thought I saw a slender, shadowy figure bending over the bed. The figure turned as I came in, put a finger to its lips, and vanished; and Trisha woke and held out her arms to me. I put my face down on her warm, drowsy, petal-soft cheek, and stayed there with her. The presence of love was all around me, and filled my heart. "I was dreaming," she said. I didn't need to ask her of whom.

The children accepted Kathleen's absence without surprise: they asked no questions; they remembered her only with joy. Later on, when they were older, and in another place, she began to merge in their minds with Trina, and then I found them talking about things that had happened "when Mommy was here"—such as the wedding, and the picnic on the beach.

I stayed away from the beach at first, hating the ocean, and not able to bear the sight of Kathleen's empty house. But when the healing set in, I took to going to the little house myself, and more and more often. I found a comfort in it, as though love still warmed the bare rooms; and sometimes, when I'd been there a while, I could almost see them as they used to be, with the curtains drawn at the windows, and the screens and the shells. At such times she seemed near me, and yet less than the air around me.

Now, when I worked at my book, Trisha sat with me and cut her paper dolls, and Chris played by himself in the yard. The work went slowly; mostly I sat and stared out of the window at the sea. No daemon spoke to me, or guided my thoughts beyond myself to better worlds.

My friends were gentle with me, they tried to take me out of myself, but I had no desire to see anybody. There wasn't anything I could say to them, there wasn't any way to explain what had happened to me, or how I felt. Perhaps Uncle Harry Cole might have understood, but he was away on a fishing trip up north. Once again, as before, there was no one to talk to.

That was the way things were the night the hills caught fire.

A Santana, the strong, dry wind from the desert, had been blowing all day, scattering sand and dust across the Coast Highway, and bending the tops of the eucalyptus. The fire must have started about midnight, in one of the canyons; and it swept outward and downward, and it went fast.

I was asleep when I thought I heard someone calling me. It sounded like Trina's voice, very far away; and then the sound of the sea was in it, and then it was Kathleen's voice, and I woke in the darkness, and there was nothing there.

I could see a murky glow through my window, and I got up and went to the door and looked out. The whole line of hills back of the house was on fire, with flames licking the crest, and falling in golden streams through the canyons. I could smell the smoke, and see the sparks explode into the sky as the eucalyptus went up, and the pine. It was a big fire, and I didn't know where it would go. The low, glittering, snake-like lines of flame extended as far as I could see.

I went in to wake the children. It was four o'clock. "We'd better get out," I said.

We didn't take much with us, there wasn't time. We piled a few things into the car—a blanket, some clothes, and a few treasures; Trisha took her sea-horse, and Chris the little fishing spear Kathleen had given him. I took the branch of coral from the mantlepiece, and a picture of Trina.

We drove south through the smoke and the smell of burning, with the low, steady roar of the fire in our ears, watching the hills blaze up behind us and the sparks float like stars across the highway on their way to the sea. The children sat wrapped in their blanket, shivering in the night cold; Chris whimpered once or twice, but Trisha looked around her with eyes like saucers. I remember thinking it was lucky that Uncle Harry Cole hadn't been home in Nichols Canyon.

We were well past Las Flores when I remembered that I'd left my manuscript in my desk. It was too late to go back for it. The fire engines and the police cars passed us, going in, their sirens wailing and their headlights blazing at us through the dark. Perhaps if I hadn't had the children with me, I'd have gone back anyway, but I couldn't risk it.

At Topanga the sheriffs were stopping northbound cars, and turning them back. It was a big fire.

We found room in a motel at Santa Monica and stayed there the rest of the night and the next day, and after that the Bassets took us in. They were very kind. We never spoke of Kathleen; I knew they thought she had deserted me.

It was several days before the fire was out and the roads clear, and we were able to drive home again, past the scorched fields and the burned-out canyons with their black, twisted trees. The air was still smoky with the fire-smell, and here and there we could see the blackened timbers of houses on the hills. Beyond Malibu the flames had reached the sea in several places; Paradise Cove had been swept, and the moors beyond Trancas.

We got to our own house at last, and it was gone; and there was nothing left of the little house on the beach but charred wood and broken tile. Sparks must have come over in the wind and set fire to the roof, and nothing could have saved it. Nothing remained of the summer but what I could remember, a branch of coral, and a fishing spear.

Trisha cried a little, but Chris was stoic about it. "We had a good time in that old house," he said. "I baked a cake," said Trisha, "and I gave a party. And I was sick, and Mommy came." "You mean Kathleen," said Chris: "Kathleen came."

We left the beach, and went to live in Sierra Madre near the mountains. Perhaps my children would get to know the mountains the way they knew the sea.

My book was gone with the house, but it didn't matter; I had a different story to write now, for I knew there was still wonder in the world. Wonder and benediction.

It was in Sierra Madre that I found a copy of the strange wedding ceremony the minister had used to marry Dick and Alice. It was in a little-known work by Bernard of Trèves, translated by Ben Ray Redman. The minister hadn't read all of it, for after the line "So love returns, to love," there was another paragraph.

"These Beings," Bernard had written, "are indeed Sendings, for they are sent to the Beloved to take the place of one gone from his side. But being not of Mortal Flesh, for them to love as a mortal is forbidden; and such taking place, they must find themselves recalled into the Element from which they came."

A NOTE ON THE AUTHOR

ROBERT NATHAN *was born in New York City in 1894, and was educated at private schools in the United States and Switzerland. While attending Harvard University he was an editor of the* Harvard Monthly, *in which his first stories and poems appeared.*

Except for two short periods during which he was a solicitor for a New York advertising firm and a teacher in the School of Journalism of New York University, Mr. Nathan has devoted his time exclusively to writing. He is the author of some thirty-six volumes of poetry and prose, and from this body of distinguished work he has acquired a reputation as a master of satiric fantasy unique in American letters. He lives now in California with his wife.

A NOTE ON THE TYPE AND PRODUCTION

The text of this book is set in Caledonia, a Linotype face designed by W. A. Dwiggins (1880–1956), who was responsible for so much that is good in contemporary book design. Though much of his early work was in advertising and he was the author of the standard volume Layout in Advertising, *Mr. Dwiggins later devoted his prolific talents to book typography and type design, and worked with great distinction in both fields. In addition to his designs for Caledonia, he created the Metro, Electra, and Eldorado series of type faces, as well as a number of experimental cuttings that have never been issued commercially.*

Caledonia belongs to the family of printing types called "modern face" by printers—a term used to mark the change in style of typeletters that occurred at the end of the eighteenth century. It is best evidenced in the letter shapes designed by Baskerville, Martin, Bodoni, and the Didots.

This book was composed, printed, and bound by H. Wolff, New York. The paper was made by S. D. Warren Company, Boston, Mass. Typography based on designs by W. A. Dwiggins.